W9-AAJ-792

James Burks

FOR DAVE GROHL—WHO INSPIRES ME TO CREATE AND LIVE LIFE TO THE FULLEST. THANK YOU!

AN IMPRINT OF PENGUIN RANDOM HOUSE LLC, NEW YORK

FIRST PUBLISHED IN THE UNITED STATES OF AMERICA BY RAZORBILL, AN IMPRINT OF PENGUIN RANDOM HOUSE LLC, 2022

VISIT US ONLINE AT PENGUINRANDOMHOUSE.COM.

LIBRARY OF CONGRESS CATALOGING-IN-PUBLICATION DATA
NAMES: BURKS, JAMES (JAMES R.), AUTHOR, ILLUSTRATOR.
TITLE: MIND CONTROL! / JAMES BURKS.
DESCRIPTION: NEW YORK : RAZORBILL, 2022. | SERIES: AGENT 9 | SEQUEL TO: FLOOD-A-GEDDON! | AUDIENCE: AGES 8-12 YEARS |
SUMMARY: AGENT 9 IS FORCED TO TEAM UP WITH A NEW PARTNER TO TAKE ON A SEEMINGLY UNSTOPPABLE NEW FOE: A ROGUE AGENT WHO KNOWS EVERY TRICK IN THE S4 BOOK.
IDENTIFIERS: LCCN 2021055634 | ISBN 9780593202975 (HARDCOVER) | ISBN 9780593202999 (TRADE PAPERBACK) | ISBN 9780593202982 (EBOOK) | ISBN 9780593205822 (EBOOK) | ISBN 9780593205815 (EBOOK)
SUBJECTS: CYAC: GRAPHIC NOVELS. | SPIES—FICTION. | HUMOROUS STORIES. | LCGFT: SPY COMICS. | HUMOROUS COMICS. | GRAPHIC NOVELS. CLASSIFICATION: LCC PZ7.7.B83 AG 2022 | DDC 741.5/973—DC23/ENG/20211123 LC RECORD AVAILABLE AT HTTPS://LCCN.LOC.GOV/2021055634

MANUFACTURED IN CHINA

10 9 8 7 6 5 4 3 2 1

TOPL

TWO DAYS AGO...
KRACKOW

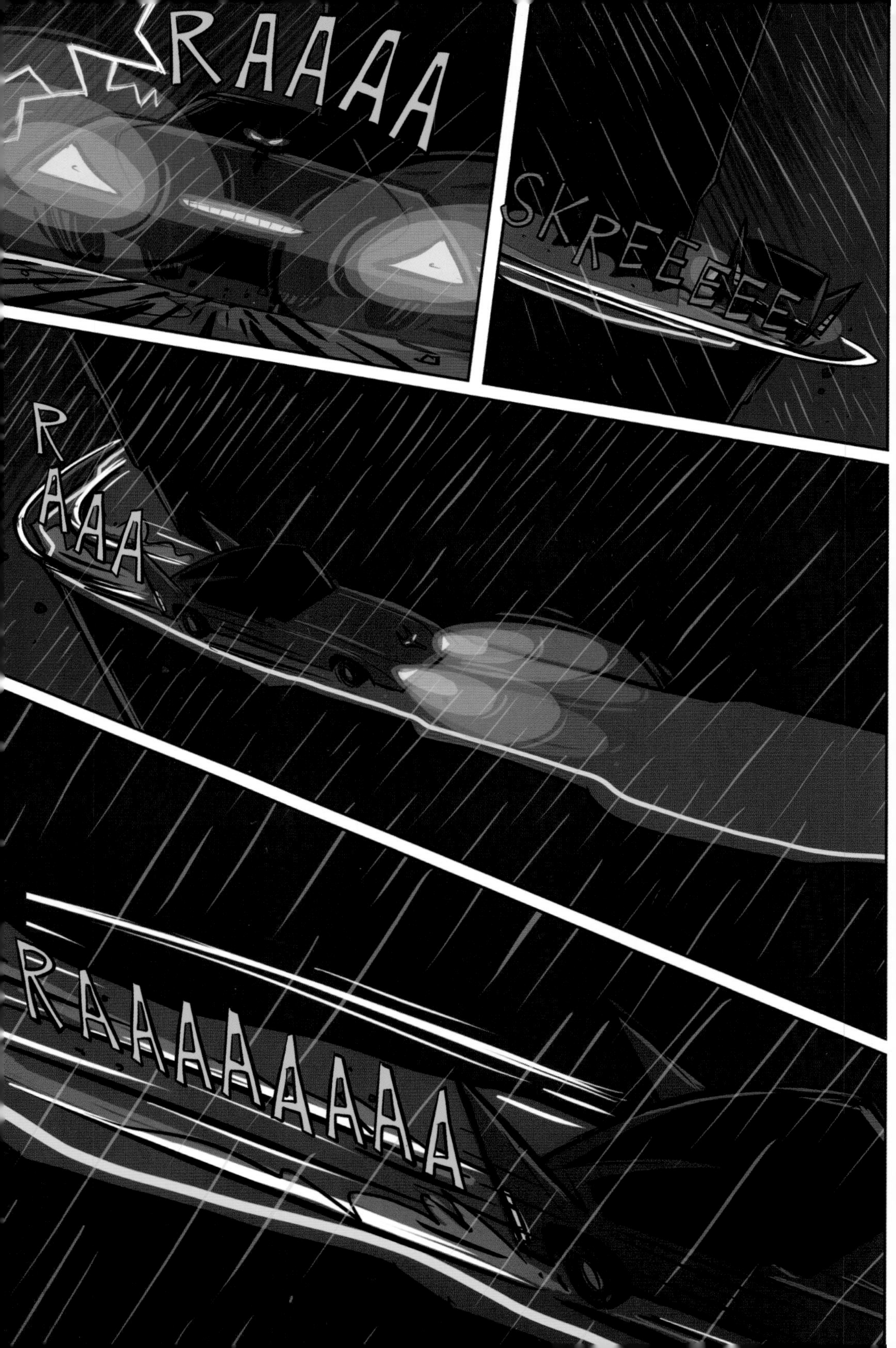
RAAAAA
SKREEEEEE
RAAAA
RAAAAAAAAA

RUMBLE
RAAAA
KRACKOW
BLAST

SPLASH
RAAAAA
RAAAAAA

SWERVE
RAAAA
RAAAAAA

RAAAAAA
RAAAAAAAAA
SKREEEECH

DIVISION—SECRET LAB

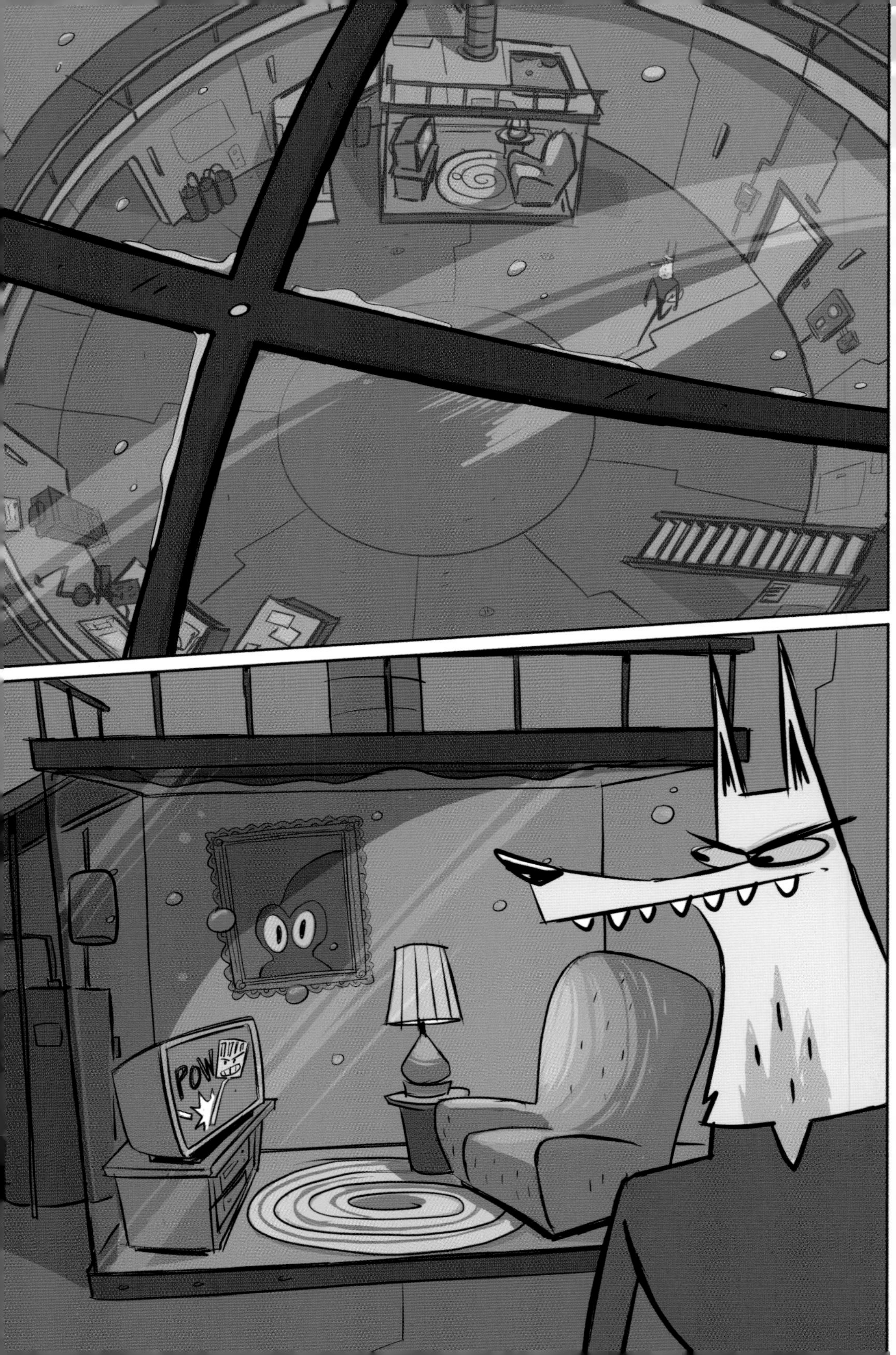
POW

INSTITUTE OF MAD SCIENTISTS
certifies that
IQ
has successfully completed the program of
MANIACAL MECHANISMS
and
DOOMSDAY DEVICES
and is hereby awarded the title of
MAD SCIENTIST
IMS

MIND-CONTROL DEVICE (MCD)

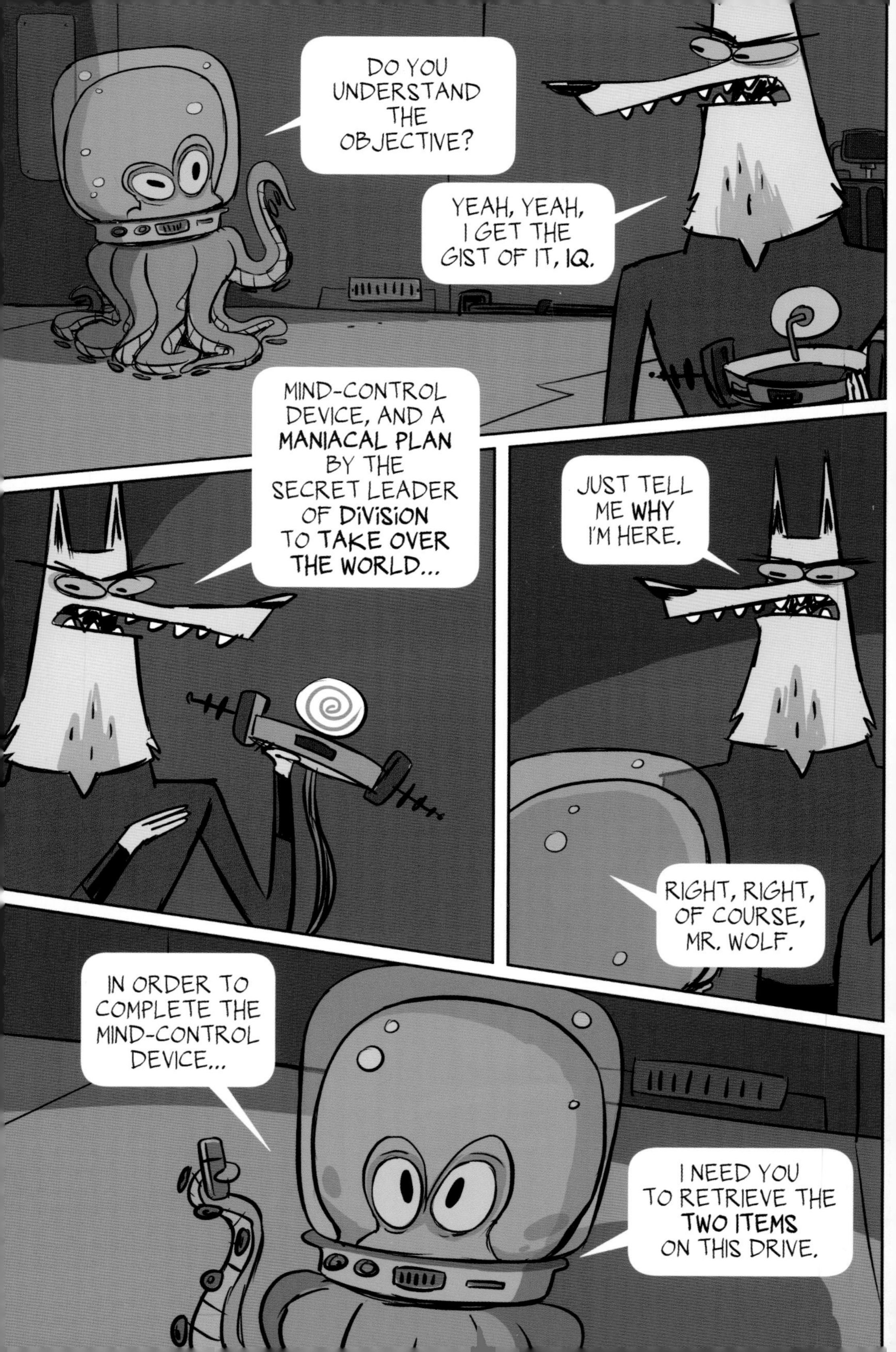
DO YOU UNDERSTAND THE OBJECTIVE?
YEAH, YEAH, I GET THE GIST OF IT, IQ.
MIND-CONTROL DEVICE, AND A MANIACAL PLAN BY THE SECRET LEADER OF DIVISION TO TAKE OVER THE WORLD...
JUST TELL ME WHY I'M HERE.
RIGHT, RIGHT, OF COURSE, MR. WOLF.
IN ORDER TO COMPLETE THE MIND-CONTROL DEVICE...
I NEED YOU TO RETRIEVE THE TWO ITEMS ON THIS DRIVE.

GREAT. AND MY PAYMENT?
YES, ABOUT THAT...
AFTER YOU SUCCESSFULLY—
AFTER?!
LET ME MAKE TWO THINGS CLEAR.
ONE—I NEVER FAIL.
AND TWO—I ALWAYS TAKE MY PAYMENT UP FRONT!
CERTAINLY. WHAT WAS I THINKING?

OBVIOUSLY I WASN'T THINKING.
PLOP PLOP PLOP PLOP PLOP
PLOP
I'VE GOT YOUR PAYMENT RIGHT HERE.
SAFE AND SOUND.
FILED UNDER Y FOR "YOU'RE THE BEST!"
HERE YA GO.
TWO MILLION, AS REQUESTED.

OH, AND, UH...
I NEED TO INFORM YOU THAT...
...AGENT NINE RESCUED THE SUPER-SECRET SPY SERVICE, AND THEY'RE BACK IN OPERATION.
DON'T WORRY.
I HAVE PLANS FOR S4...
AND THEIR SO-CALLED AGENT NINE!
DING

PRESENT DAY...

FORTY THOUSAND FEET IN THE AIR...

THERE'S NO BETTER MID-FLIGHT SNACK THAN A FISH-FLAVORED YOGURT CUP.
MMMMMM.
BEOOP.
I'M SUPER EXCITED TOO, FIN. I CAN'T WAIT TO FIND OUT WHAT OUR NEXT MISSION WILL BE.
MAYBE WE'LL GET TO THWART AN ALIEN INVASION.
OR SAVE THE QUEEN!

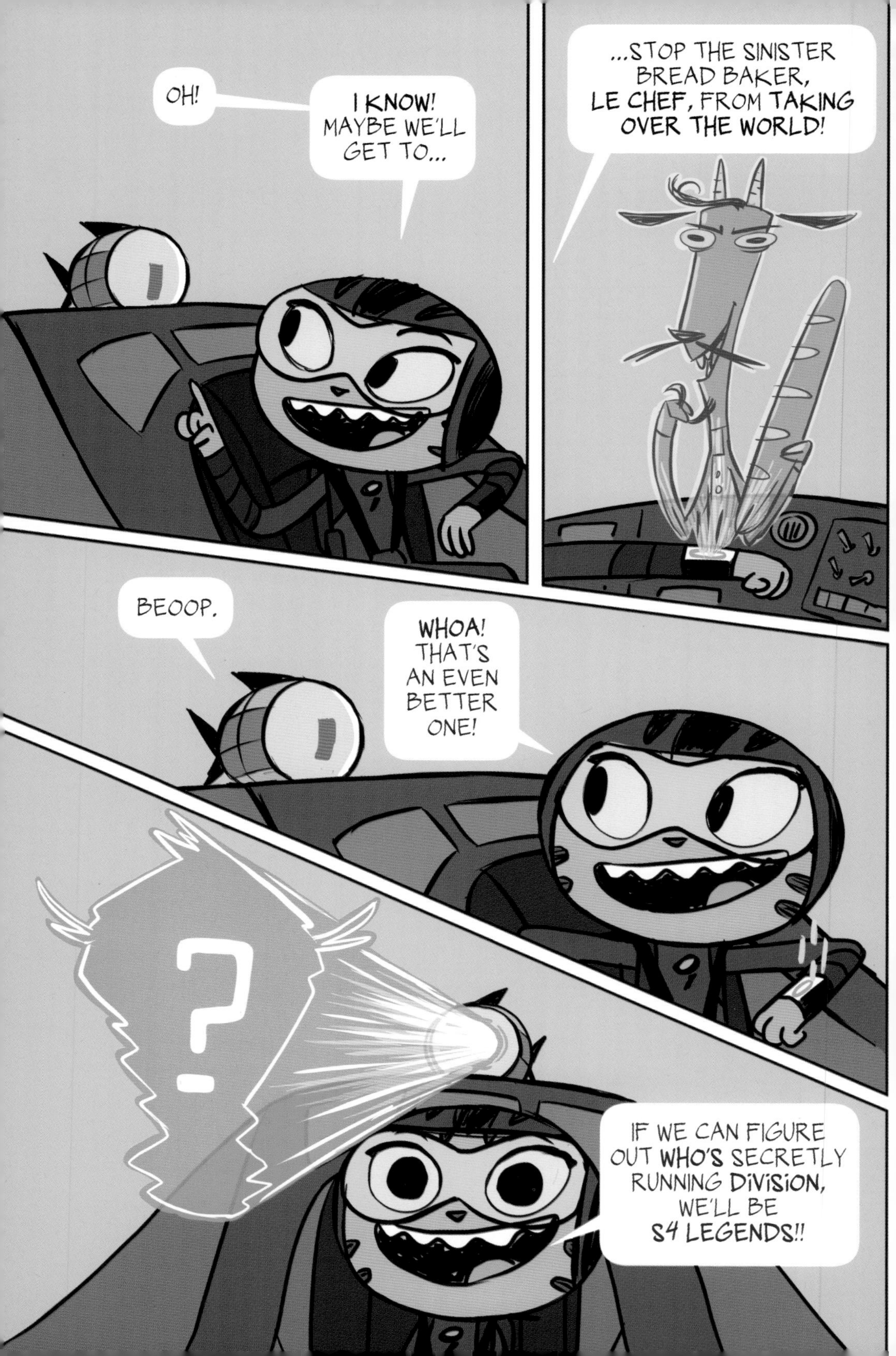
OH!
I KNOW! MAYBE WE'LL GET TO...
...STOP THE SINISTER BREAD BAKER, LE CHEF, FROM TAKING OVER THE WORLD!
BEOOP.
WHOA! THAT'S AN EVEN BETTER ONE!
?
IF WE CAN FIGURE OUT WHO'S SECRETLY RUNNING DIVISION, WE'LL BE S4 LEGENDS!!

AND MAYBE EVEN ACHIEVE OUR ULTIMATE GOAL OF BEING NAMED...
SPY OF THE MONTH!

BZZZZ

BZZZ

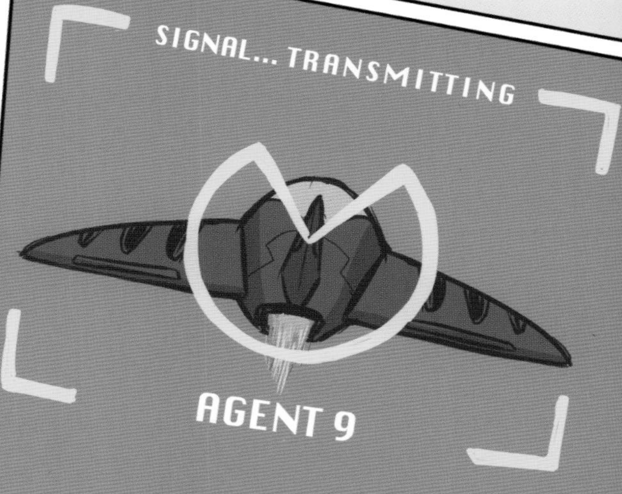
SIGNAL... TRANSMITTING
AGENT 9

WHAT DO YOU SAY WE THROW THIS BABY INTO OVER-OVERDRIVE AND GET TO HEADQUARTERS AHEAD OF SCHEDULE?
BEOOP!
HOLD ON TO YOUR GIGABYTES!
WRRRRR
OVER-OVERDRIVE
OVERDRIVE
DRIVE
VRRRRRR
WHOOOOOOSH

SIGNAL... TRANSMITTING
BZZT
BZZT
AGENT 9
BZT

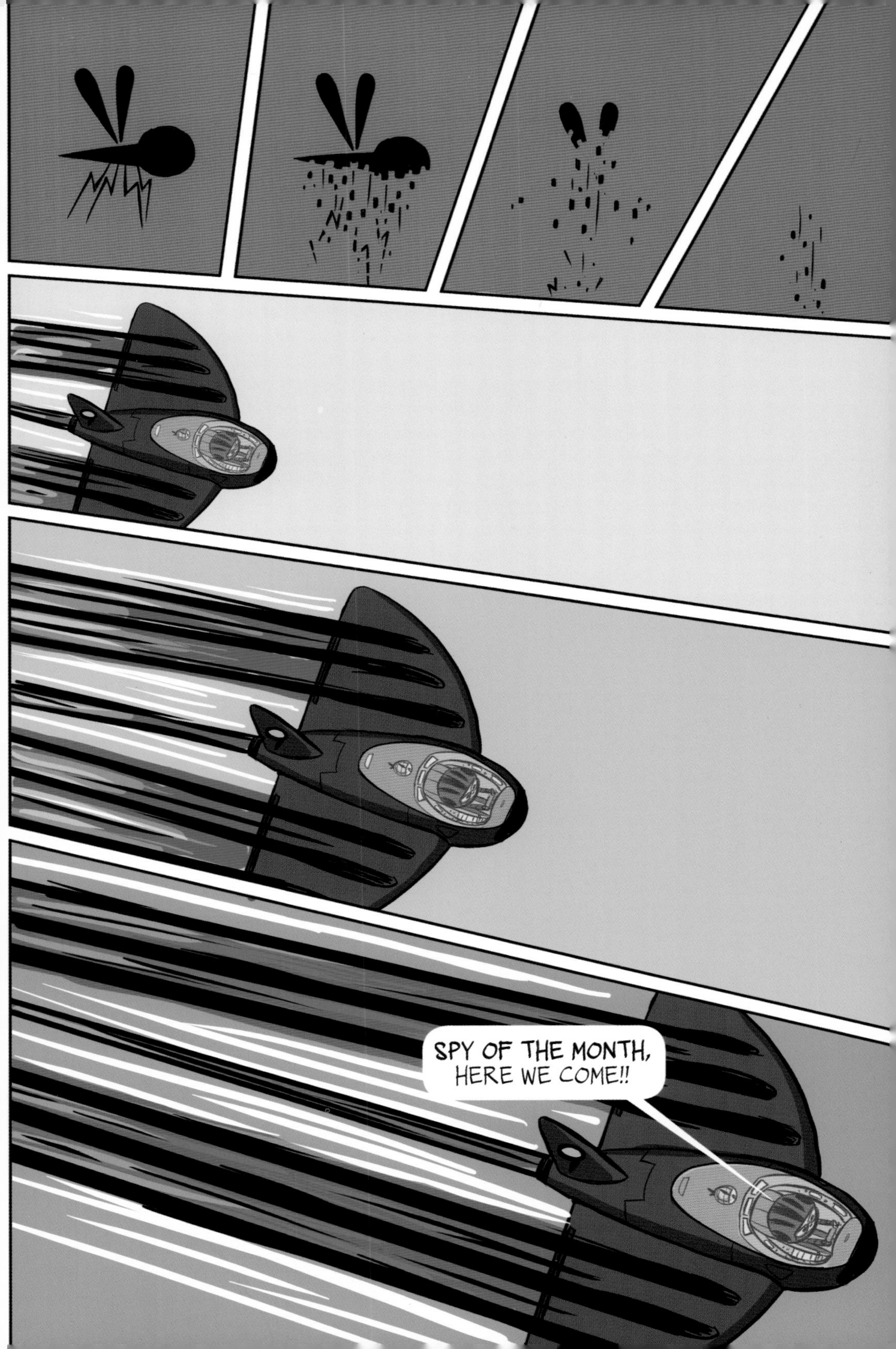
SPY OF THE MONTH,
HERE WE COME!!

SEVEN MILES FROM CONTINENTAL CITY
YUCK'S
PICKLED BRUSSELS SPROUTS

YUCK'S
PICKLED BRUSSELS SPROUTS
BZZ
BZZZOOOOOW

WRRRR
S4 HEADQUARTERS

S4

OH, HEY, THIS IS NEW.
BUZZ
HALT.
STOP!
S.W.A.R.M.* SECURITY CHECKPOINT
* SURVEILLANCE WARNING AERIAL RECONNAISSANCE MONITORS
LOOKS LIKE THEY'VE INCREASED SECURITY SINCE OUR LAST VISIT.
SCANNING...
BING
AGENT 9... CLEAR!
BUZZ BUZZ BUZZ.
YOU MAY PROCEED.
IT'S BEE-N A PLEASURE BEE-ING SCANNED BY YOU.
BEE-OOP.
SECURITY CHECKPOINT

UNDERCOVER DEPT.
YIKES!
I FEEL SORRY FOR THE POOR SOUL WHO HAS TO WEAR THAT.

LISTENING IN PROGRESS
ECHO, HOW GOES THE SNOOPING?
YOU KNOW HOW IT IS. SAME OLD, SAME OLD.
SNOOPING DEPT.

PROGRESS
SOMEONE'S ALWAYS PLANNING TO TAKE OVER THE WORLD.
I'LL DO MY BEST TO MAKE SURE THAT DOESN'T HAPPEN.

WHAT'S-IT-CALLED DEPT.
BEOOP.
OPERATION NAMES:
• BRAIN RE-PROGRAMMER
• THOUGHT CHANGER
- WHAT WAS I THINKING?
- MIND CONTROL
- MIND NOT MINE
• MIND IF I TAKE OVER YOUR MIND?
- BRAIN CHANGE
CODENAME:
PICKLE
ELBOW
FISH STICK
NOSE
I GUESS IT WOULD BE FUN TO COME UP WITH COOL MISSION NAMES.
BUT THEN WHO'S GOING TO SAVE THE WORLD IF WE DON'T? WE HAVE A RESPONSIBILITY TO UPHOLD.
PLUS, WE'D NEVER ACHIEVE THIS!
SPY OF THE MONTH
TOP SECRET

SPY OF THE MONTH
TOP SECRET
IMAGINE HOW GREAT WE'RE GOING TO LOOK IN **TOP-SECRET** SILHOUETTE.

TOP SECRET
IT'S **GOING** TO HAPPEN, FIN!

I CAN FEEL IT!

SPLAT

BEOOP.
IT SURE DOES LOOK LIKE THEY ADDED A FINGERPRINT SCANNER SINCE OUR LAST VISIT.

BEEP

HOW'S IT GOING, E?

FIN.
AGENT 9.
O'S BEEN EXPECTING YOU.

HEY, CAN YOU GIVE US ANY SECRET INSIDER INFO ABOUT OUR NEXT MISSION?
I COULD, BUT...

...THEN I'D HAVE TO WIPE YOUR MEMORY, LOCK YOU IN A VAULT, DROP THAT VAULT IN THE DEEPEST PART OF THE OCEAN, AND GUARD IT WITH RAZOR-TOOTHED PIRANHAS.

JUST KIDDING...
HA-HA.

THERE WOULDN'T BE ANY PIRANHAS—THEY'RE A **FRESHWATER** FISH.

NEVER MIND. I'M SURE O WILL GIVE US ALL THE DETAILS.

I'LL BE HERE IF YOU CHANGE YOUR MIND.

AGENT 9, YOU MADE IT, AND YOU KEPT YOUR SHIP IN ONE PIECE TOO.
THERE'S A **FIRST TIME** FOR EVERYTHING, O.

I'M READY TO PROVE THAT I'M THE **BEST** AGENT IN S4.
25

NO MORE DISTRAC—

WHOA! IS THIS NEW?
25 YEARS OF PERFECT SERVICE
GRAB

25 YEARS OF PERFECT SERVICE

THAT'S JUST SOMETHING THEY GIVE OUT WHEN YOU **NEVER** MISS A DAY OF WORK.
25 YEARS OF PERFECT SERVICE

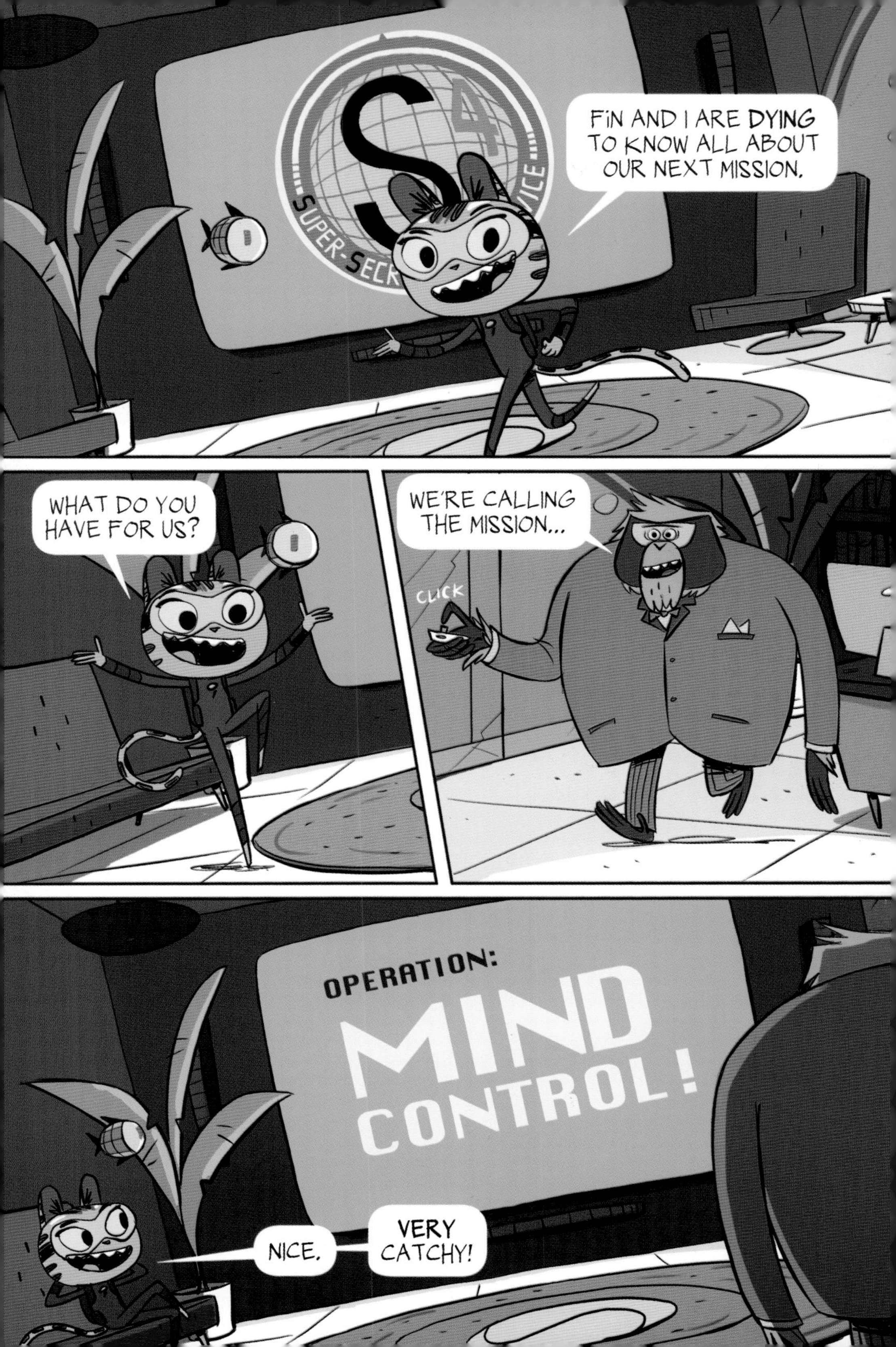
SUPER-SECR
FIN AND I ARE DYING TO KNOW ALL ABOUT OUR NEXT MISSION.
WHAT DO YOU HAVE FOR US?
WE'RE CALLING THE MISSION...
CLICK
OPERATION:
MIND CONTROL!
NICE.
VERY CATCHY!

AGENTS IN OUR SNOOPING DEPARTMENT RECENTLY **INTERCEPTED** THIS CODED MESSAGE FROM **DIVISION.**

CLICK

IYZJAWNHUYKILHAPAPSKEPAIONA
MQENAZLNKPKAHAYPNKIWCJAPWJ
ZMQWNGJWJKPAYGXWPPANUSKHB
WYPERWPAZ—EM

AS I WAS SAYING... WE WERE ABLE TO DECIPHER THE MESSAGE...
CLICK
MCD NEARLY COMPLETE. TWO ITEMS REQUIRED: PROTO ELECTROMAGNET AND QUARK NANOTECH BATTERY. WOLF ACTIVATED.—IQ
...AND FROM THIS PIECE TOGETHER DIVISION'S DEVIOUS PLAN.

LAY IT ON ME. MY EARS ARE SET TO RECEIVE!

WE BELIEVE DIVISION SCIENTIST IQ IS BUILDING A MIND-CONTROL DEVICE, OR "MCD," AS INDICATED IN THE CODED MESSAGE.
CLICK

WHICH, IF COMPLETED, WOULD GIVE DIVISION THE POWER TO TURN WHOEVER THEY CHOOSE INTO UNWILLING PUPPETS AND CAUSE CHAOS AROUND THE GLOBE.

THAT IS WHY THE MISSION IS CALLED "MIND CONTROL!"
IT'S ALL MAKING SENSE NOW.
WHOA!
WHO'S THAT?
THAT'S THE WOLF.
AN INDEPENDENT OPERATIVE WHO WORKS FOR WHOEVER HAS THE MOST MONEY.
LOOKS AND SOUNDS LIKE TROUBLE TO ME.
YOU DON'T KNOW THE HALF OF IT.

I'VE HAD PROBLEMS WITH THE WOLF IN THE PAST.
HE MUST NOT BE UNDERESTIMATED.
MENTAL NOTE MADE.

DIVISION HAS HIRED THE WOLF TO RETRIEVE TWO ITEMS.
CLICK

THE FIRST IS THIS.
PROTOTYPE SUPERCONDUCTING ELECTROMAGNET
4x THE POWER AND A QUARTER THE SIZE OF A STANDARD S-E

WHICH WILL BE ON DISPLAY AT...
RAIL-CON
3 DAYS ON A TRAIN
LOADED WITH...
- GUEST SPEAKERS
- FUTURE TRAIN TECH
- TRAIN FOOD
- TONS OF TRAIN FUN
TICKETS ON SALE NOW!

BEOOP?
MAGNETS POWER BULLET TRAINS.
THAT MAGNET CAN QUADRUPLE THE SPEED OF THE FASTEST TRAIN.

OR, IN THE **WRONG** HANDS, IT CAN BE USED TO CREATE A POWERFUL MIND-CONTROL DEVICE.

WHAT WE NEED YOU TO DO, NINE...

...IS SWITCH OUT THE PROTOTYPE WITH THIS **DECOY** BEFORE THE WOLF CAN STEAL IT.

THAT SEEMS EASY ENOUGH.

IT'S NOT QUITE AS EASY AS IT LOOKS.

A **HALF TON** OF SAPPHIRE GLASS COVERS THE ELECTROMAGNET, WHICH **YOU** WILL HAVE TO LIFT TO MAKE THE SWITCH.

I'VE BEEN WORKING OUT, SO IT **SHOULDN'T** BE A PROBLEM.
HRRAH!
YEEAHH!
MRRRAH!

OH. SORRY. THEN WHAT HAPPENS AFTER THE SWITCH?
SLIDE
SLIDE

ONCE THE WOLF STEALS THE DECOY...
...YOU'LL TRACK HIM TO IQ'S SECRET LAB...
...TRANSMIT THE COORDINATES BACK TO S4...

...AND THEN WE'LL SEND IN ADDITIONAL SUPPORT TO HELP FINISH THE JOB.
ANY QUES—
WHICH...

...WILL BRING FIN AND ME CLOSER TO IDENTIFYING THE SINISTER SUPER-SECRET HEAD OF DIVISION AND BEING NAMED...
SPY OF THE MONTH!

LET'S KEEP OUR FOCUS ON THIS MISSION FOR NOW.

RIGHT! FOCUS. AND WHAT ABOUT THE SECOND ITEM?
SNAP

THE SECOND ITEM IS A NANOTECH BATTERY CREATED BY QUARK LABS.
COMPACT SIZE
INFINITE POSSIBILITIES
UNLIMITED POWER
CLICK

BUT WITHOUT A WORKING ELECTROMAGNET, THE MCD WILL BE USELESS.
SO YOU ONLY NEED TO KEEP YOUR EYES ON THE WOLF WHILE HE RETRIEVES THE BATTERY.
GOT IT!
I'LL SNEAK INTO RAIL-CON...
...MAKE THE SWITCH...

...TRAIL THE WOLF...

...FIND THE SECRET LAB...
...AND GET THE MCD!
WORLD SAVED!
MISSION ACCOMPLISHED!
I LIKE YOUR ENTHUSIASM, BUT THIS MISSION IS TOO IMPORTANT TO REST ON THE SHOULDERS OF ONLY ONE AGENT.
I COULDN'T AGREE MORE. THAT'S WHY I HAVE FIN.

I DON'T DOUBT THAT FIN IS A VALUABLE ASSET TO EVERY MISSION YOU GO ON, NINE.

BUT IT'S **IMPORTANT** YOU LEARN TO **TRUST** OTHERS AS WELL.

WHAT?! FIN AND I MAKE THE **PERFECT** TEAM!

WE EVEN **FINISH** EACH OTHER'S...

YOU'RE SUPPOSED TO SAY "**SENTENCES.**"

BEOOP.
SEE?! "SENTENCES." NO OTHER AGENTS REQUIRED.

IT'S NOT UP FOR DEBATE, AGENT 9.

COME ON. YOU TRAINED ME TO BE SELF-SUFFICIENT.

TO HANDLE THINGS ON MY OWN AND—

AND NOW I REALIZE THAT MIGHT HAVE BEEN A MISTAKE.

A GOOD AGENT NEEDS TO KNOW WHEN TO ASK FOR HELP AND WORK WITH A TEAM.

I HAVE NO INTEREST IN BEING GOOD. I WANT TO BE THE BEST!

AND TO DO THAT, YOU **NEED** TO SURROUND YOURSELF WITH THE **BEST TEAM.**

BUT—
MY DECISION IS **FINAL.**

EITHER **WORK** WITH ANOTHER AGENT, OR **I WILL** ASSIGN SOMEONE ELSE IN YOUR PLACE.

FINE... I'LL DO IT.

GOOD. I THINK YOU'RE GOING TO LIKE YOUR NEW PARTNER.
BOOP

AGENT 9, MEET TRAPS.
HI!
SHE'S AN EXPERT AT GETTING INTO AND OUT OF SECURE FACILITIES, SETTING TRAPS...
WHOOP.
STILL TURNING.
COMING AROUND.
...AND A MASTER WHEN IT COMES TO TRACKING.
WHOA.
THAT MAKES YOU DIZZY.
I'M ALSO PRETTY GOOD AT KNITTING.

I MADE THIS BEANIE.
I COULD KNIT ONE FOR YOU TOO.

MATCHING UNIFORMS! WHAT DO YOU SAY?
NO. THANKS.

I'M REALLY LOOKING FORWARD TO WORKING WITH YOU.

WELP. THERE GOES SPY OF THE MONTH.

SUPER-SECRET SERVICE
OH, AND ONE MORE THING.
25
DID YOU CHANGE YOUR MIND ABOUT THE WHOLE TEAM THING?
NO.
I FORGOT TO MENTION THAT THIS IS A **COVERT OPERATION.**
YOU **MUST** KEEP A LOW PROFILE.
DON'T WORRY, O. I'VE ALREADY GOT IT COVERED.

THE NEXT DAY...
CONTINENTAL CITY STATION

WELCOME...
RAIL-CON ATTENDEES!
R-C

IS THIS DISGUISE BRILLIANT OR WHAT?

WE CAN GO WHEREVER WE WANT, AND NO ONE WILL EVEN KNOW WE'RE HERE.

LET'S HURRY UP AND MAKE THE SWITCH SO WE CAN GET OUT OF THIS RIDICULOUS COSTUME.
IT SMELLS HORRIBLE.

OH, THAT'S JUST THE CHEESE I BROUGHT FOR A SNACK. YOU WANT SOME?
NO. I DON'T.

YOU SURE? IT'S SHARP CHEDDAR. IT'LL KEEP YA SHARP.

LISTEN, I'M USED TO WORKING ALONE, AND I THINK IT'LL BE A LOT EASIER IF YOU FOLLOW MY LEAD. OKAY?

OH, YEAH, SURE. YOU WON'T EVEN KNOW I'M HERE.

I'LL BE QUIET AS A MOUSE.

NUM-NUM-NUM.

BEOOP.
RIGHT. THE MISSION. YOU'LL LOCATE THE WOLF WHILE I MAKE THE SWITCH.

YOU MEAN, "WE."

LET'S GET MOVING.
IT'S MISSION TIME.

WHOA.

WHERE'S THE TRAIN?
I CAN'T SEE.
BZZZZ

SIGNAL... TRANSMITTING
HEAT SCAN...
AGENT 9
BZZZZZ

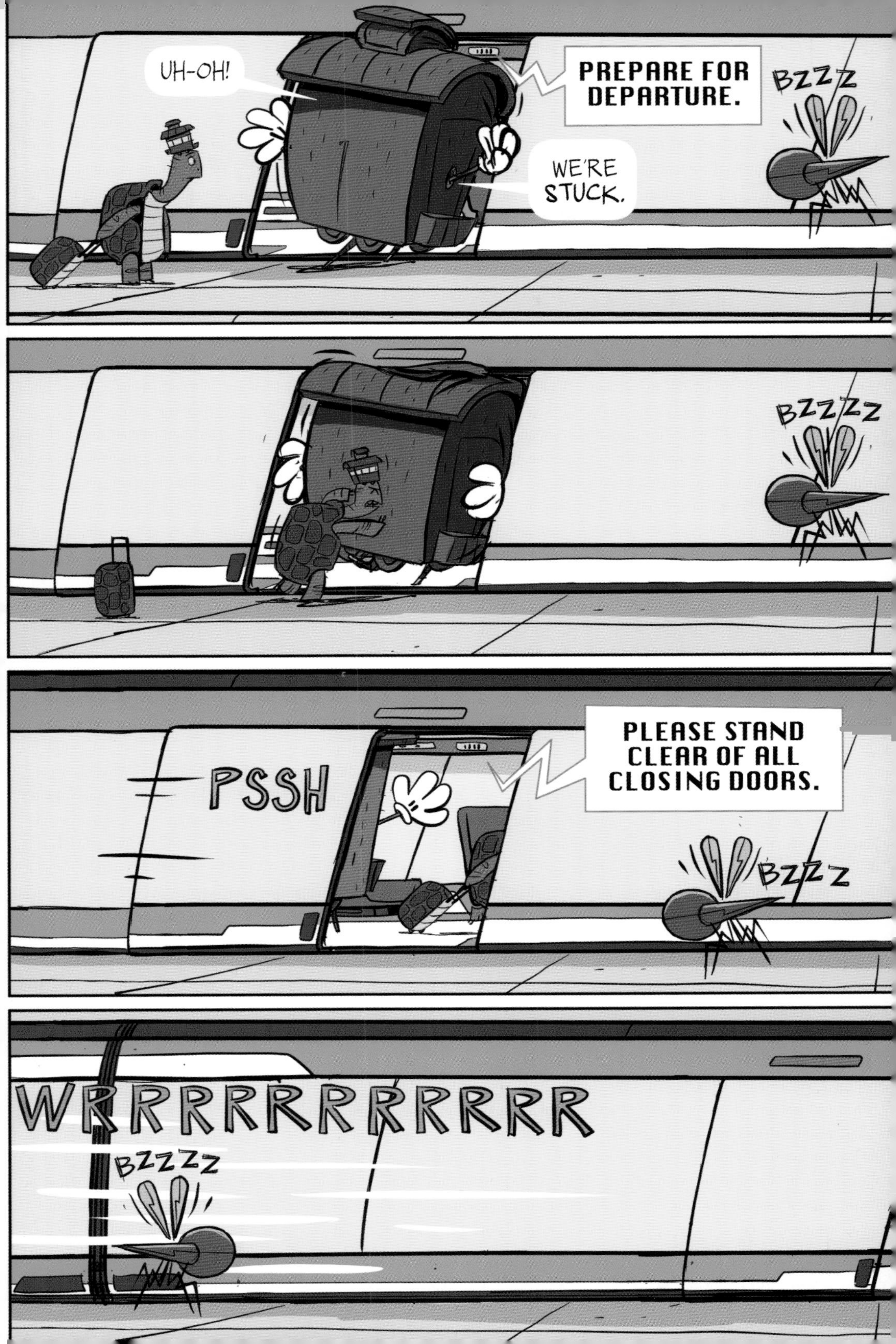
UH-OH!
PREPARE FOR DEPARTURE.
BZZZ
WE'RE STUCK.
BZZZZ
PSSH
PLEASE STAND CLEAR OF ALL CLOSING DOORS.
BZZZ
WRRRRRRRRRRR
BZZZZ

WRRRRRRRRR
ZZZ

YOU COULDN'T HAVE PICKED SOMETHING...

RRR
...I DON'T KNOW... **SMALLER** AND **EASIER** TO MOVE AROUND IN, **INSIDE A TRAIN**?
YOU MAKE A **VALID** POINT.
ONE THAT I WILL **DEFINITELY** TAKE INTO CONSIDERATION WHEN PICKING A DISGUISE FOR OUR **NEXT** MISSION.

NOPE.
NOPE.
NOPE.
ONCE WE COMPLETE THIS MISSION, WE **WON'T** BE WORKING TOGETHER AGAIN.

UNLESS I CHANGE YOUR MIND.
THE CHANCE OF THAT IS **ZERO**.

NOT THE WOLF
SEARCHING...

WRRRRRRRRRRR

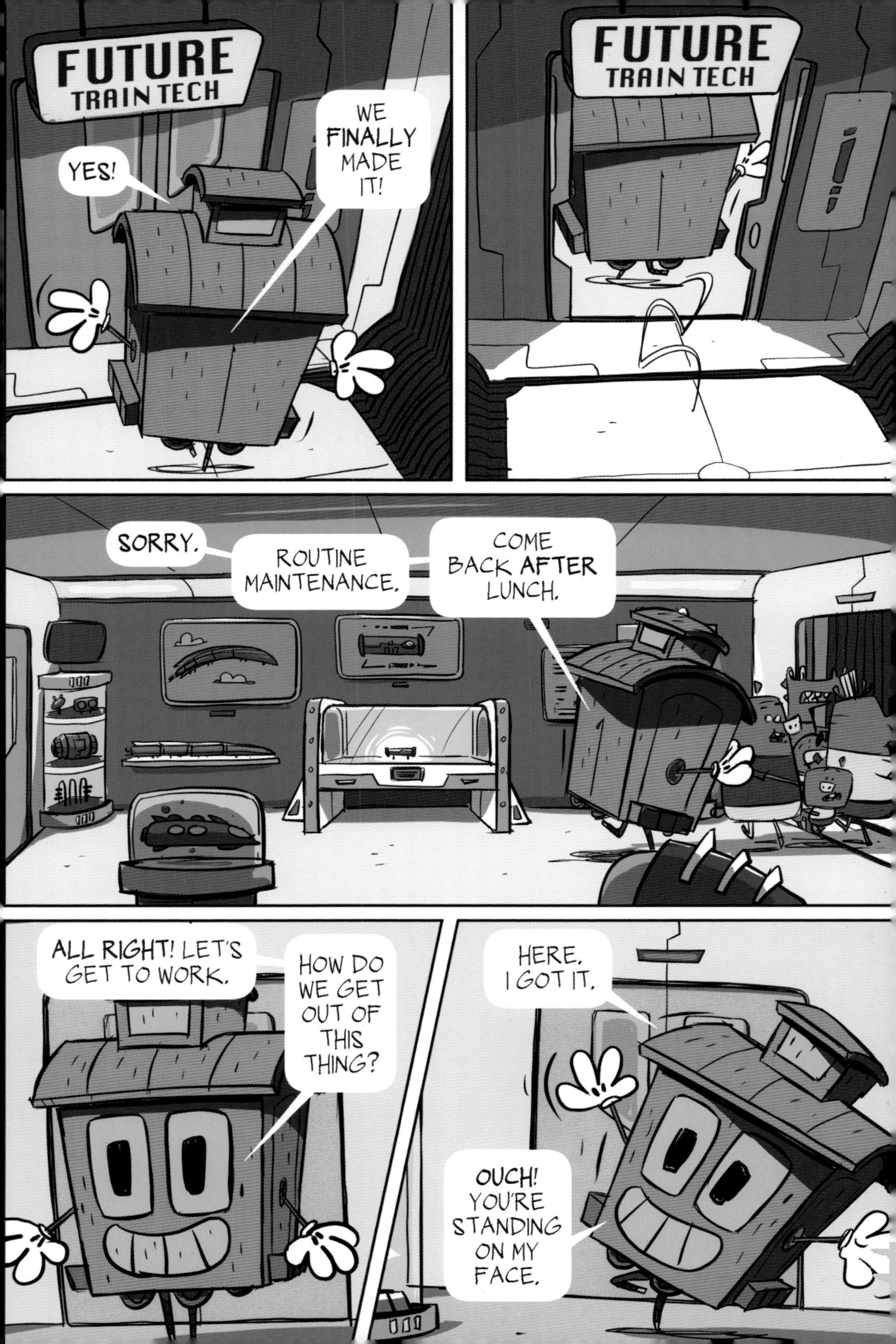
FUTURE TRAIN TECH
YES!
WE FINALLY MADE IT!
FUTURE TRAIN TECH
SORRY.
ROUTINE MAINTENANCE.
COME BACK AFTER LUNCH.
ALL RIGHT! LET'S GET TO WORK.
HOW DO WE GET OUT OF THIS THING?
HERE. I GOT IT.
OUCH! YOU'RE STANDING ON MY FACE.

THE ZIPPER IS STUCK!
WHY IS IT ALWAYS A ZIPPER?
I DON'T KNOW.
I DIDN'T DESIGN IT.
WHOA!
SPIN
YAGH!
OOF!
THUD

RRRR
RIP
GASP
PLOP
I GUESS YOU COULD SAY THAT WAS A REAL EYE-OPENER.

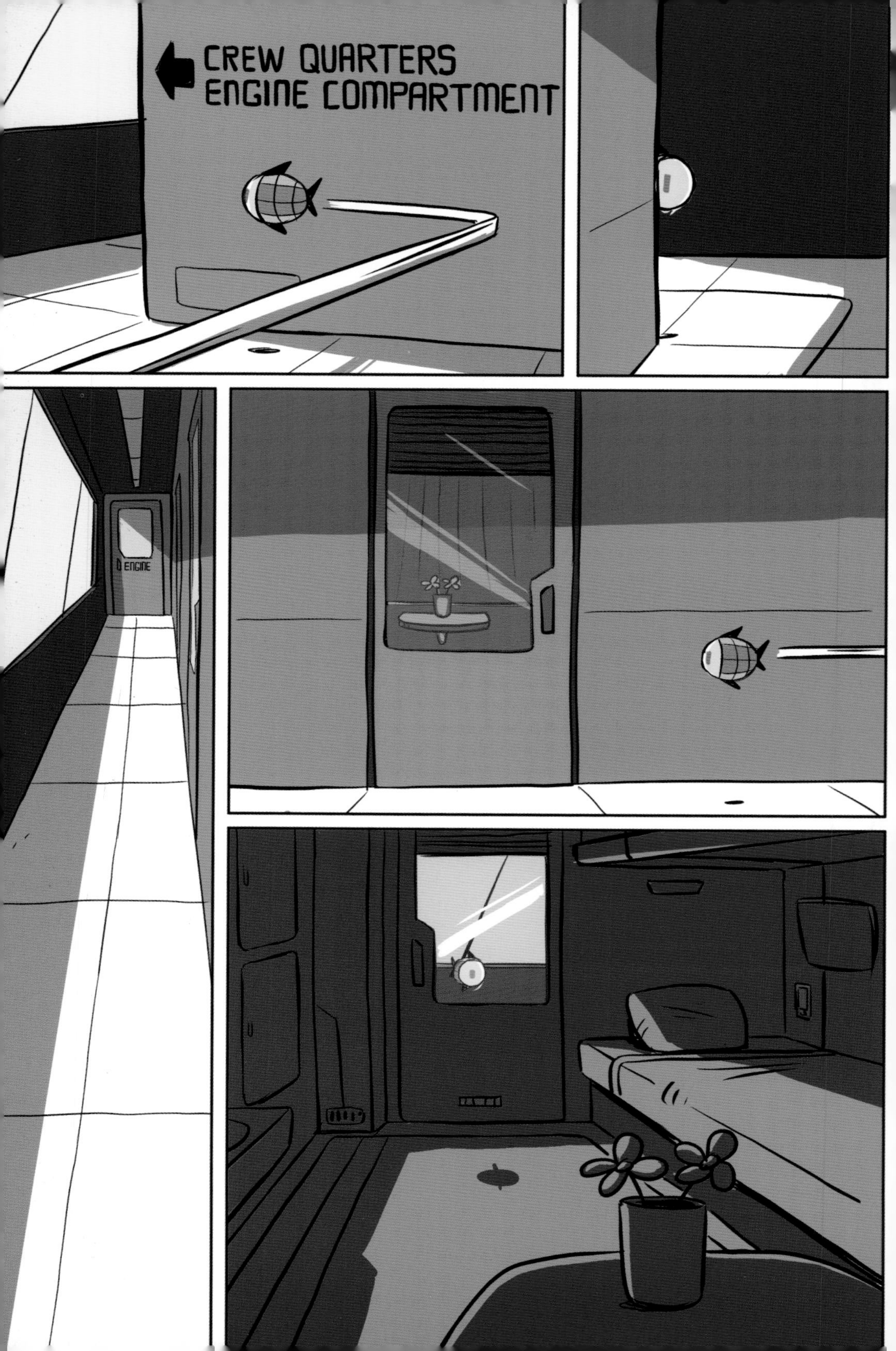

CREW QUARTERS
ENGINE COMPARTMENT
ENGINE

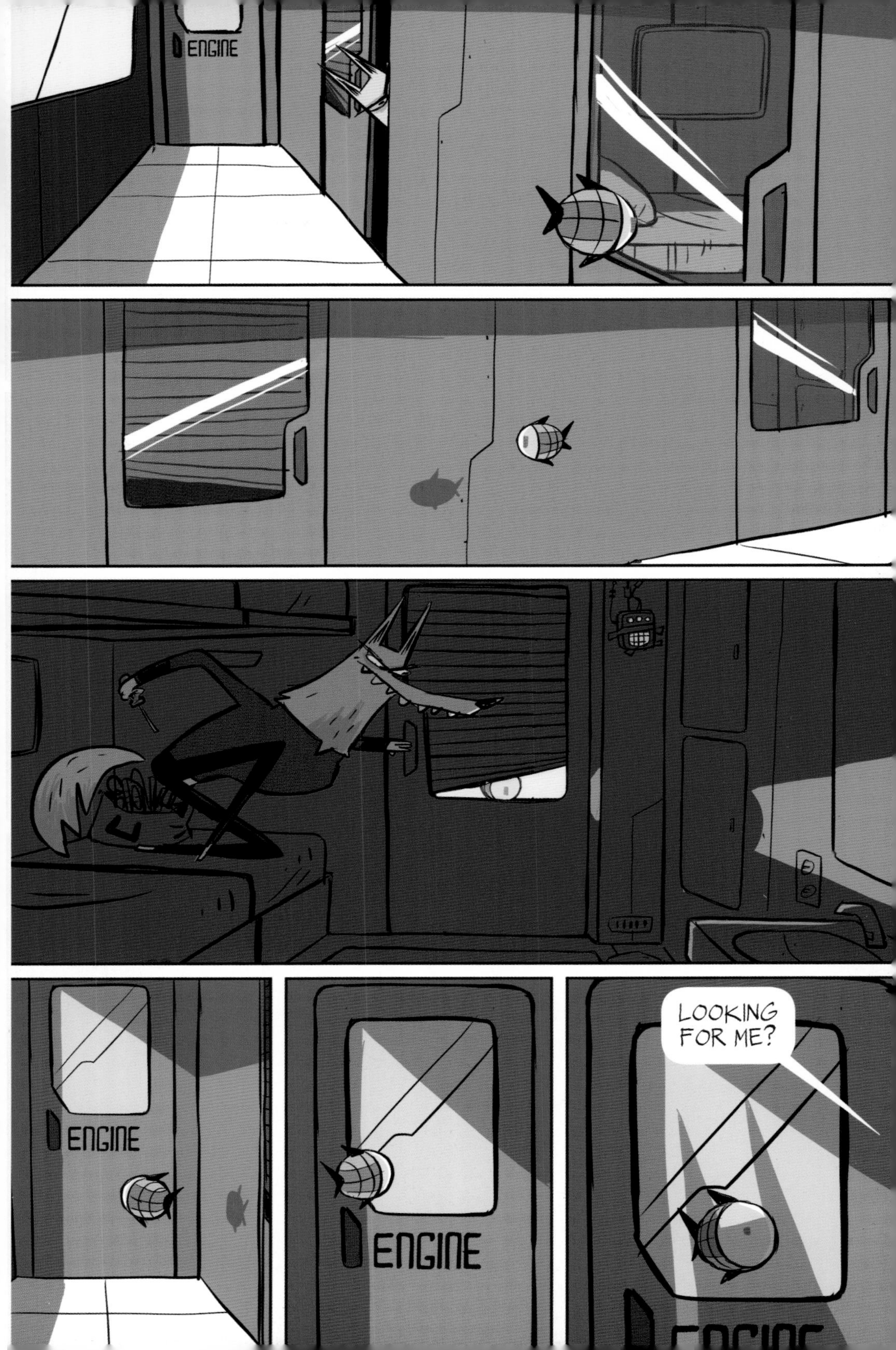
ENGINE
ENGINE
ENGINE
LOOKING FOR ME?

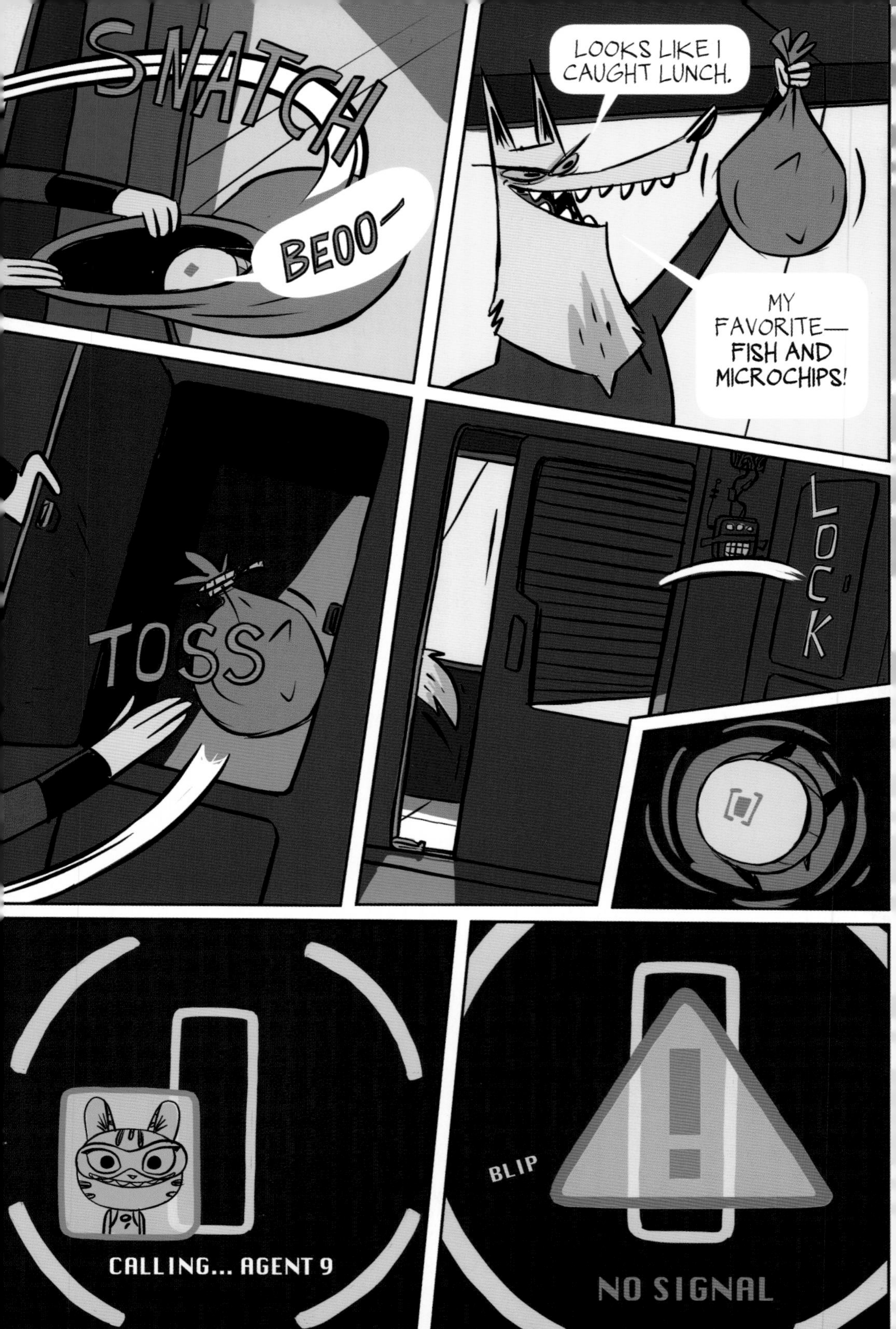
SNATCH
BEOO—
LOOKS LIKE I CAUGHT LUNCH.
MY FAVORITE— FISH AND MICROCHIPS!
TOSS
LOCK
CALLING... AGENT 9
BLIP
NO SIGNAL

FUTURE
TRAIN TECH
STICK

ARE YOU SURE YOU KNOW WHAT YOU'RE DOING?
DON'T WORRY. I GOT THIS.
I'LL HAVE THE TOP POPPED ON THIS SARDINE CAN MOMENTARILY.

AND WE HAVE LIFTOFF.
LEVITRON 3000
SLIDE
POWER

ZRRRRRRRR

PRESTO...

...CHANGO!

SUCCESS!

BZZOOOOOO...
WHAT HAPPENED TO THE LIGHTS?
WASN'T ME.

LIGHT SYSTEMS REBOOTING.
THIS DOESN'T FEEL RIGHT.
MAYBE... BECAUSE IT'S PITCH-BLACK, AND WE CAN'T SEE ANYTHING.

THE WOLF MUST HAVE HACKED INTO THE TRAIN'S COMPUTER SYSTEM.
IF HE'S COMING HERE, I'LL—
NIGHT VISION

GRAB
HUH?!
THANKS FOR DOING THE HEAVY LIFTING.
HE'S HERE!
SWIPE
WHERE? I DON'T SEE HIM.

THUD
LIGHT SYSTEMS RESTORED.
FUTURE TRAIN TECH
STAY HERE!
I CAN'T LET YOU GO BY YOURSELF!
NO! I CAN HANDLE THIS ON MY OWN!
FUTURE TRAIN TECH

CLUNK
CLUNK
BZZZZ
BZZAP
BEOOP!

WRRRR
WRRRRRRRRRRRRRRRRRR

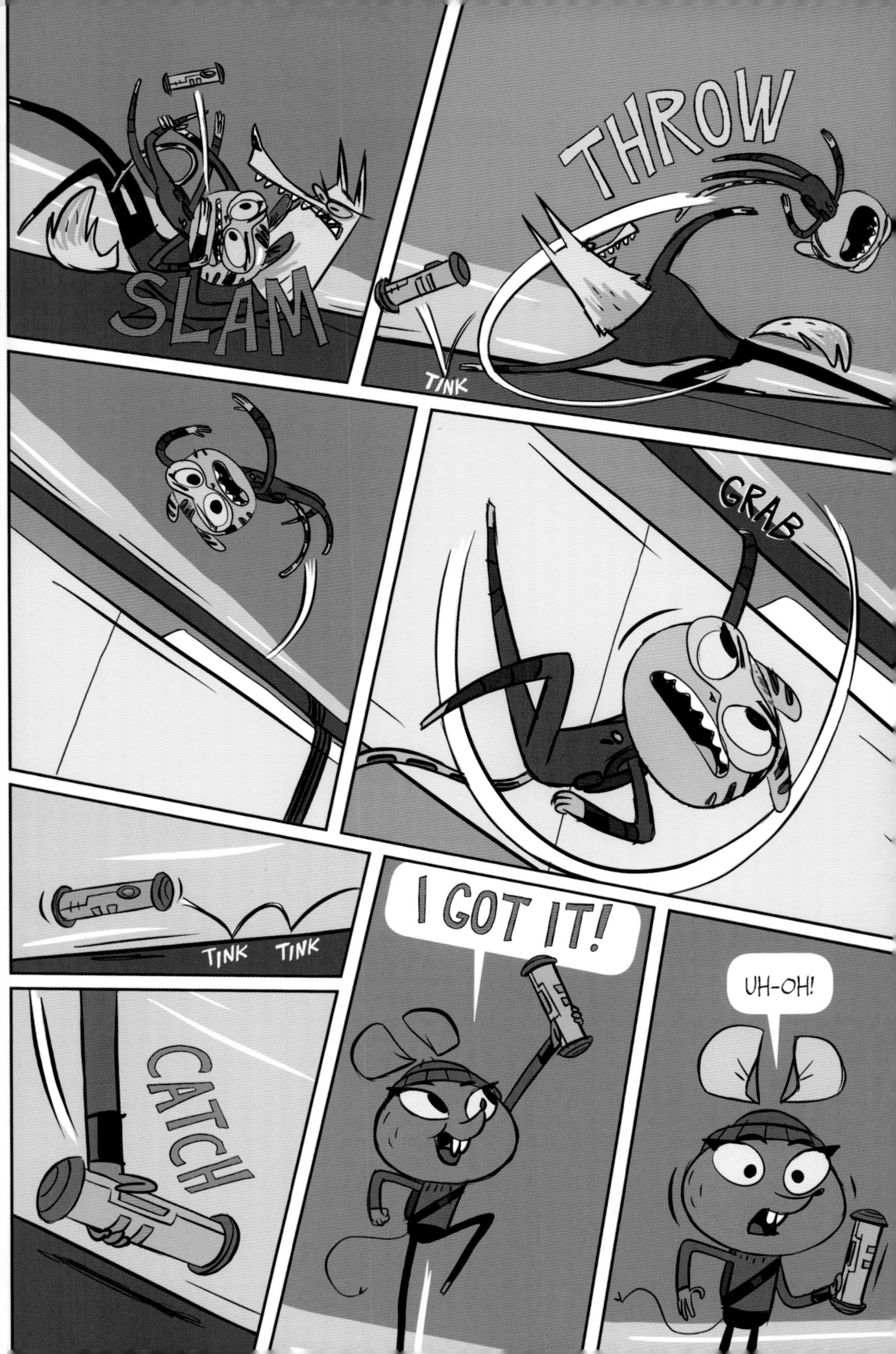
SLAM
THROW
TINK
GRAB
TINK TINK
I GOT IT!
CATCH
UH-OH!

I'LL TAKE THAT!
I'D PREFER YOU DIDN'T.
LET GO, YOU LITTLE VERMIN!
YOU DIDN'T SAY PLEASE!
GRR!
BZZZ
FIN!

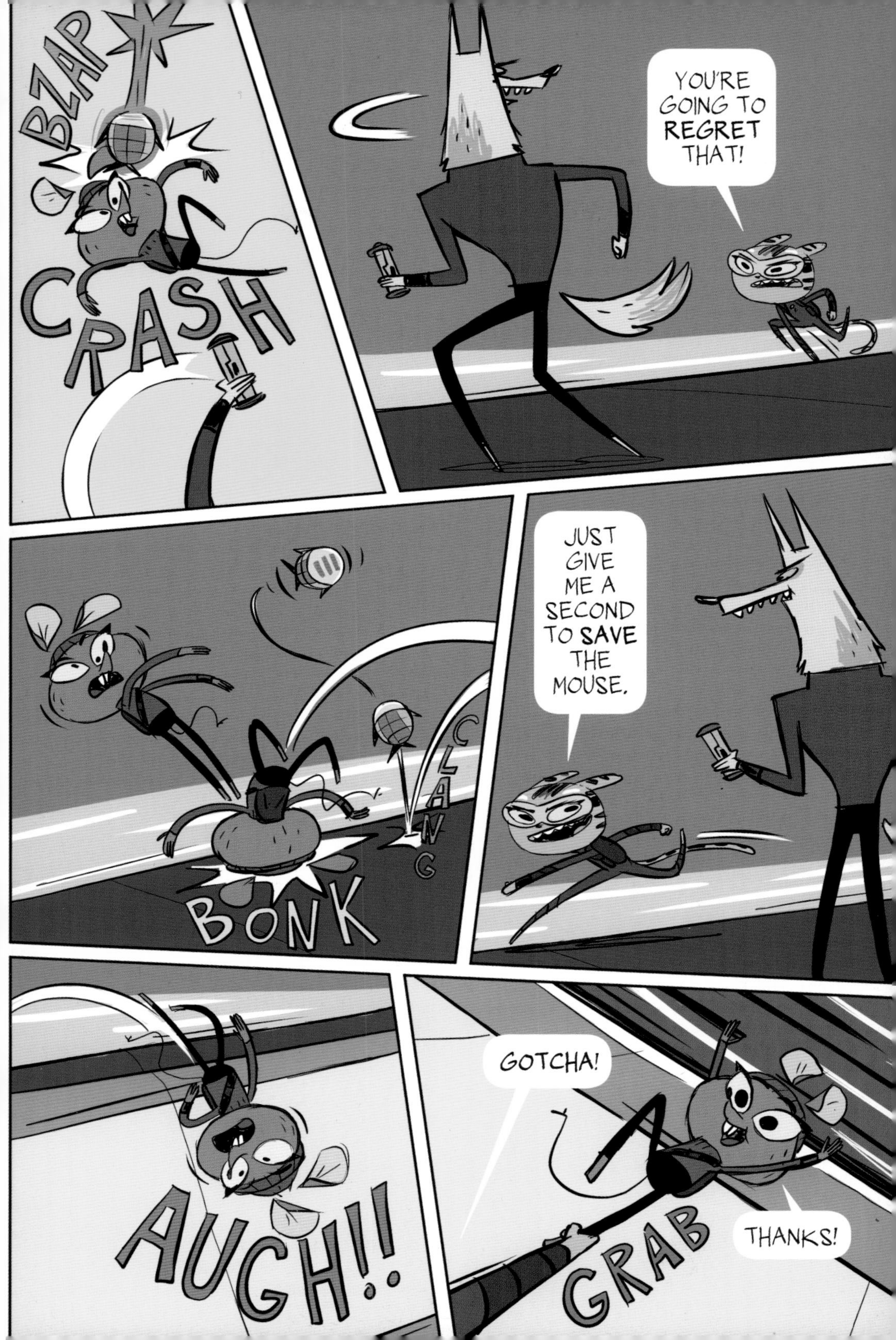
BZAP
CRASH
YOU'RE GOING TO **REGRET** THAT!
CLANG
BONK
JUST GIVE ME A SECOND TO **SAVE** THE MOUSE.
AUGH!!
GOTCHA!
GRAB
THANKS!

YOU MUST BE AGENT 9.
I'VE HEARD THRILLING TALES OF HOW TRULY SPECTACULAR YOU ARE.

OBVIOUSLY, NONE OF THEM TRUE...

...OR RETRIEVING THIS WOULD HAVE BEEN A CHALLENGE.

THAT'S FUNNY. I DIDN'T EVEN KNOW YOU EXISTED UNTIL YESTERDAY.

MAYBE YOU SHOULD GET OUT MORE.

WELL, I'D LOVE TO CONTINUE THIS **EXHILARATING** CONVERSATION...

...BUT **I'VE** GOT A BATTERY TO THIEVE...

...AND **YOU'VE** GOT A **RUNAWAY** TRAIN TO STOP.

HUH?
BEOOP?
WHAT?

DID I **FORGET** TO MENTION THE PART WHERE I **DESTROY** THE TRAIN'S OPERATING SYSTEM WITH THE **PUSH** OF A BUTTON AND SEND THE TRAIN **RACING** OUT OF CONTROL?
BOOP

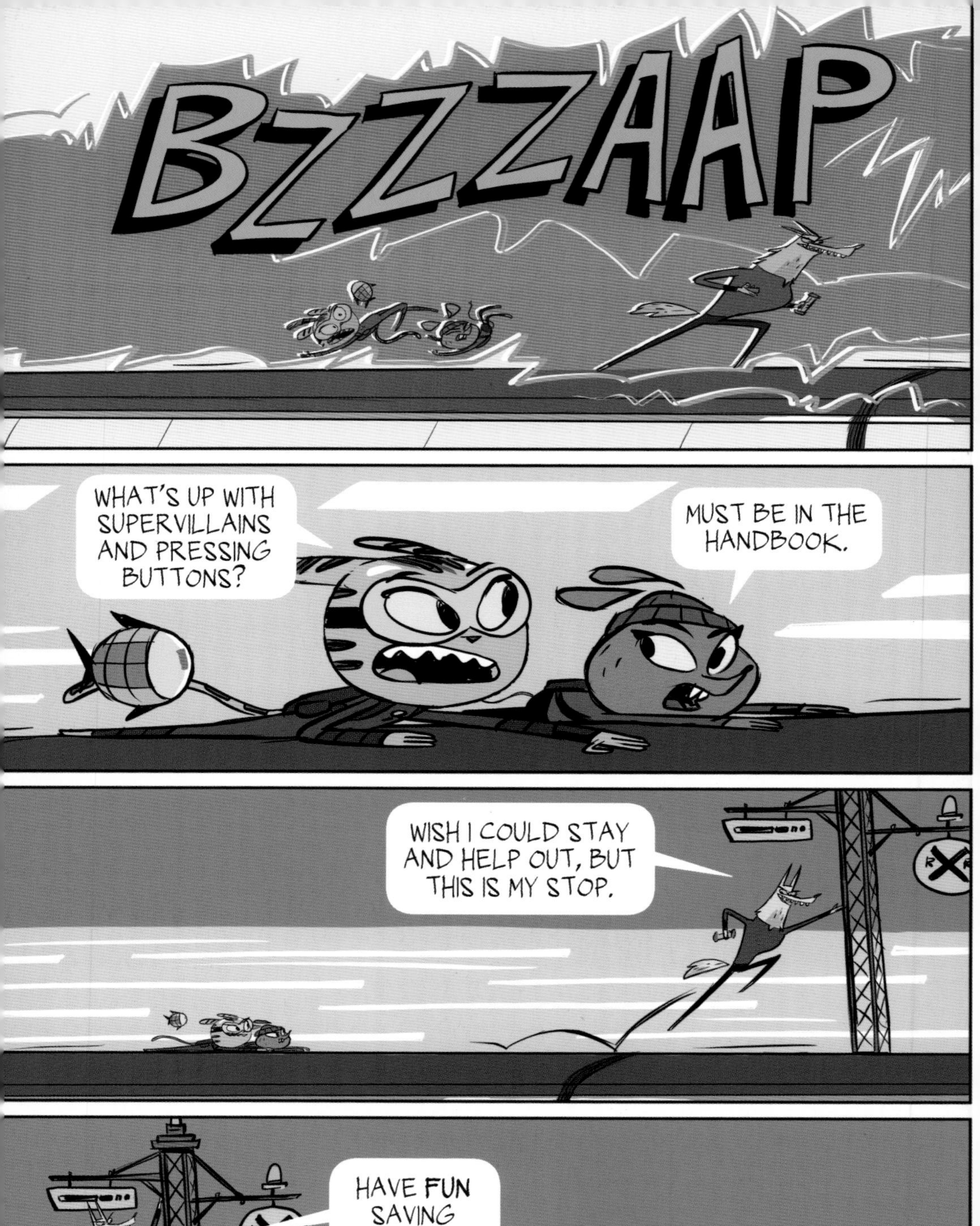
BZZZAAP
WHAT'S UP WITH SUPERVILLAINS AND PRESSING BUTTONS?
MUST BE IN THE HANDBOOK.
WISH I COULD STAY AND HELP OUT, BUT THIS IS MY STOP.

HAVE **FUN** SAVING EVERYONE!

CAN ANYTHING ELSE POSSIBLY GO WRONG ON THIS MISSION?
BEOOP.
SERIOUSLY?
WHAT DID FIN SAY?
WE HAVE TEN MINUTES TO STOP THIS TRAIN BEFORE IT CAREENS OFF THE TRACKS AT THE NEXT TURN.
BZZZ

ZOOOOOM
BLART BLART BLART BLART
THIS DOESN'T LOOK GOOD.
THERE'S NO WAY TO SHUT OFF THE ENGINE!
BLART BLART BLART BLART
REDUCE SPEED! TURN AHEAD!
BEOOP.
UH-OH!

AHEAD
ZRRR
BLART
I KNOW WHAT TO DO!
YOU DO?

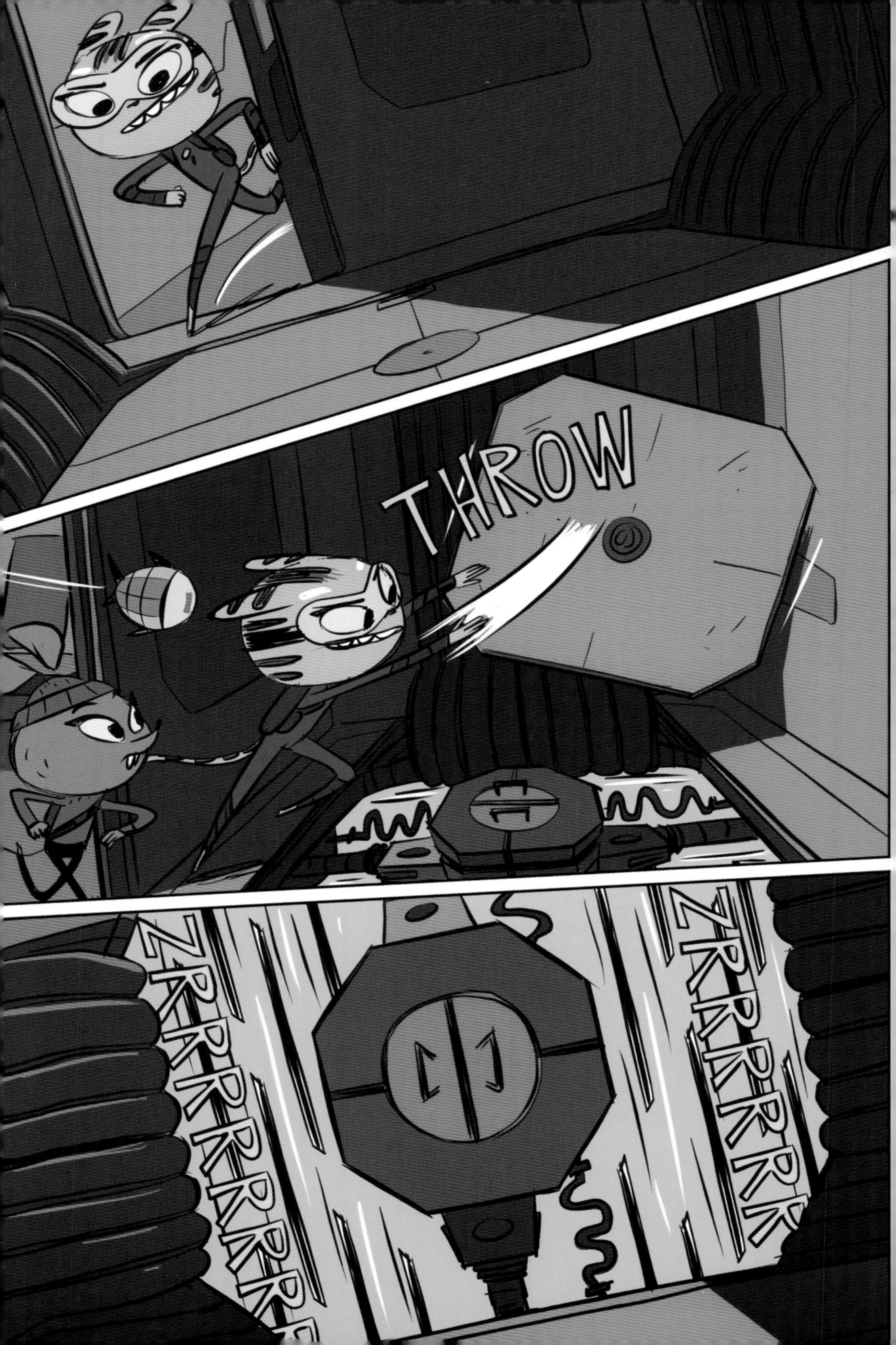
THROW
ZRRRRRRR
ZRRRRRR

DO YOU NEED HELP?
NO. I DON'T.
HRRRR!
PULL

BEOOP! BEOOP!

I KNOW! I JUST NEED A MINUTE!
PUSH

UH. I DON'T THINK WE HAVE A MINUTE!

BLART
DANGER!
BLART BLART BLAR
ZOOOOM

WHY WON'T YOU TURN?
HRRRRR!
YAAUGH!
RRRGH!
TURN
CLICK

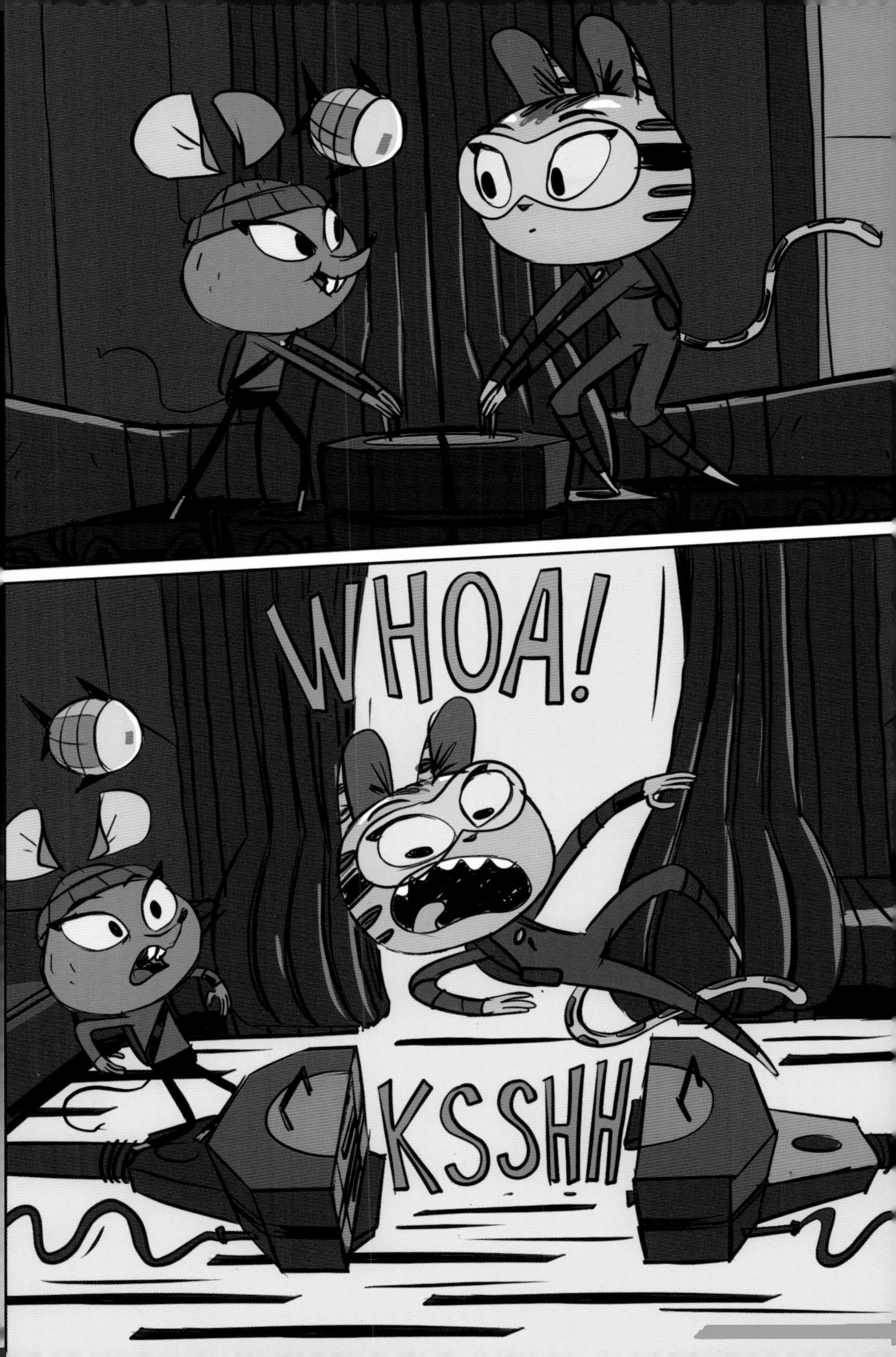
WHOA!
KSSHH

GRAB
GOTCHA!
ZZRRRRRRR
SKREEEEE

SMASH
KA-BOOM

I DON'T RECALL SEEING ANYTHING IN THE RAIL-CON PROGRAM ABOUT THE ENGINE EXPLODING. DO YOU?
NOPE. I THINK WE WOULD HAVE REMEMBERED THAT.
DOES THIS MEAN THEY WON'T BE SERVING DESSERT?

BZZZZ

WOW.
I GUESS WE COULD SAY THINGS WENT A LITTLE "OFF THE RAILS" BACK THERE.
AM I RIGHT?
NONE OF THAT WOULD HAVE HAPPENED IF YOU HAD STAYED BEHIND.

BUT NO!
INSTEAD OF STOPPING THE WOLF...

...I WAS SAVING YOU.

SORRY.
I THOUGHT YOU MIGHT NEED MY HELP.

BECAUSE, YOU KNOW...
SCRATCH SCRATCH

...WE'RE A TEAM.

YEAH, WELL, LOOK WHERE BEING A TEAM GOT US.

WE FAILED!

YAGH! THE WOLF USED US TO GET THE MAGNET.

AND NOW HE'S ON HIS WAY TO GET THE SECOND ITEM.

RUB RUB

UNLESS WE CAN GET TO IT FIRST.

HOW?!
WE'RE STRANDED IN THE MIDDLE OF NOWHERE!

BEOOP.
WE CAN'T CALL S4.

IF O FINDS OUT WE ALREADY FAILED THIS MISSION...

...IT'LL BE OUR LAST!

I CAN CALL A FRIEND WHO OWES ME A FAVOR.

I DON'T KNOW.
RUB RUB

I'M A LITTLE UNEASY ABOUT...

THE LAST TIME I TOOK A RIDE FROM A STRANGER, I ENDED UP BATTLING A GIANT OCTOPUS.

NO PROBLEM. WE CAN CALL ONE OF YOUR FRIENDS INSTEAD.

MY FRIENDS?

UHHH...
GULP

NEVER MIND... YOU CAN CALL.

HEY, IT'S TRAPS.
LISTEN, I NEED A FAVOR.
SIGH.

WHAT'S **WRONG** WITH ME, FIN?

BEOOP.

I KNOW. I **NEED** TO LEARN TO TRUST OTHERS.

IT'S A LOT **HARDER** THAN IT SEEMS.

MROW!
GOOD NEWS!

OUR LIFT IS ON THE WAY.

SORRY. DID NOT MEAN TO SCARE YOU.
WHO'S SCARED?

NOT ME.
MY CAT REFLEXES ARE ALWAYS ON HIGH ALERT.

I WAS THIS CLOSE TO ATTACKING.

FISH-FLAVORED YOGURT CUP?

WHERE'D YOU GET THIS?
I ALWAYS PACK SOME SNACKS.
S4 ALMOST CODE-NAMED ME **SNACKS** INSTEAD OF TRAPS.
DID O TELL YOU THIS WAS MY FAVORITE?

NOPE.
IT'S MY FAVORITE TOO.

MMMMMM...
I LOVE HOW IT **TASTES** LIKE THE **SEA SMELLS**.

YEP. JUST THE RIGHT AMOUNT OF SALTY GOODNESS AND—

REAL FISH FLAVOR!

ARE YOU SURE YOU DON'T WANT IT?
NO. I WANT YOU TO HAVE IT.

THANKS.

WHUP-WHUP-WHUP-WHUP-WHUP-WHUP

WHUP-
WHUP-
WHUP

WHUP-
WHUP-
WHUP

THAT'S OUR RIDE.

NICE!

WELCOME ABOARD, AGENT 9. MY NAME'S ROTORS.
NICE TO MEET YOU. WE CAN'T THANK YOU ENOUGH FOR HELPING US OUT.
CLICK
I'M ALWAYS HAPPY TO LEND A FLIPPER—OR IN THIS CASE, A HELICOPTER—TO FRIENDS IN NEED.
JUST RELAX AND ENJOY THE RIDE.

WRRRRRRRRRRRRRRR
BUZZZZ

WRRRRRRRRR
HEY, UH, LISTEN... I WANTED TO APOLOGIZE ABOUT EARLIER.

THIS WHOLE "WORKING WITH A PARTNER" THING IS NEW TO ME.

SO IT MIGHT TAKE SOME TIME, YOU KNOW, FOR ME TO ADJUST.

NO WORRIES. BY THE TIME THIS MISSION IS OVER, WE ARE GOING TO MELT TOGETHER LIKE COLBY JACK CHEESE.

DON'T YOU THINK THAT SOUNDS A LITTLE TOO CHEESY?
TOO MUCH CHEESE? THAT'S IMPOSSIBLE.

QUARK LABS

GOOD LUCK.
IF YOU EVER NEED A LIFT, YOU KNOW WHO TO CALL.
THANKS, ROTORS.
I OWE YOU ONE.
ALL RIGHT, NEW PLAN!
WE GET INSIDE, RETRIEVE THE NANOTECH BATTERY...

...AND STOP DIVISION FROM COMPLETING THE MCD!
DO YOU THINK THE WOLF IS ALREADY INSIDE?
THERE'S ONLY ONE WAY TO FIND OUT.

SCANNING
...
CLICK

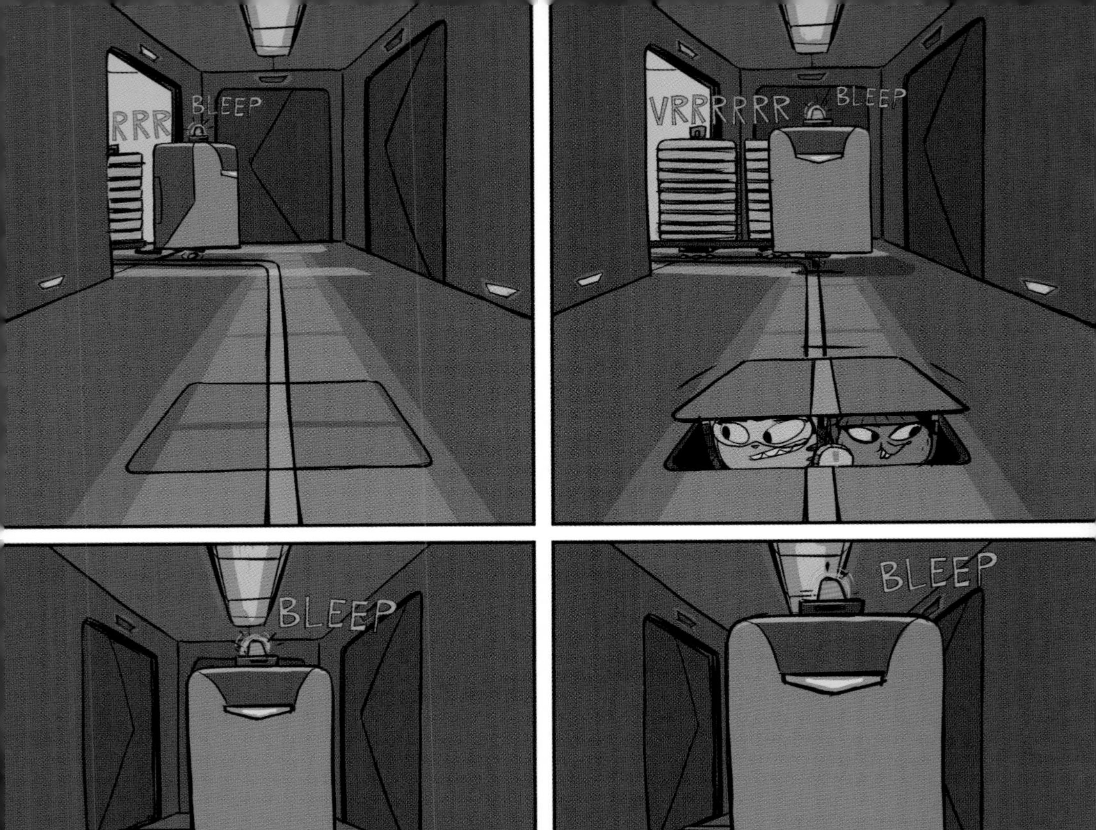
RRR
BLEEP
VRRRRRR
BLEEP

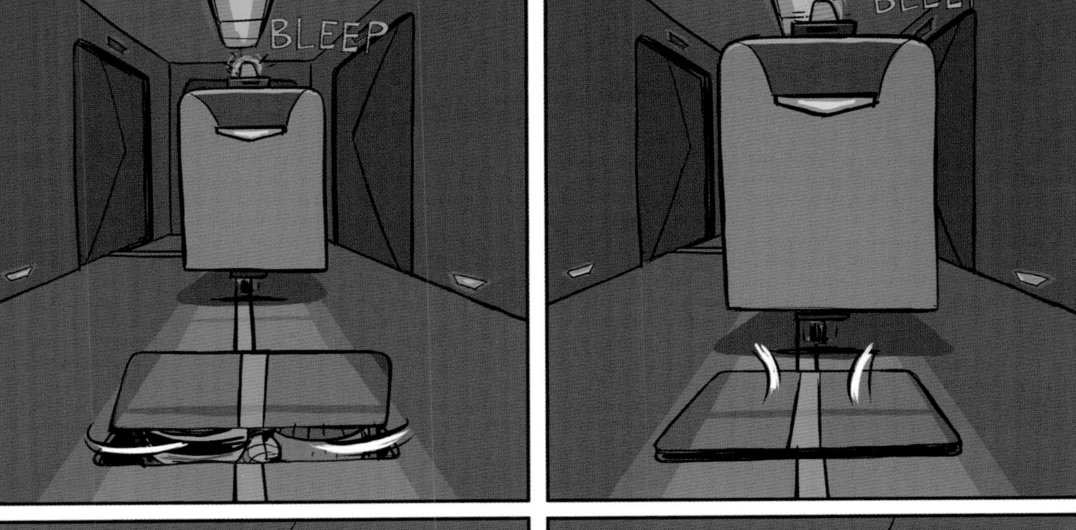
BLEEP
BLEEP

RRRR
BLEEP

VRRRRR

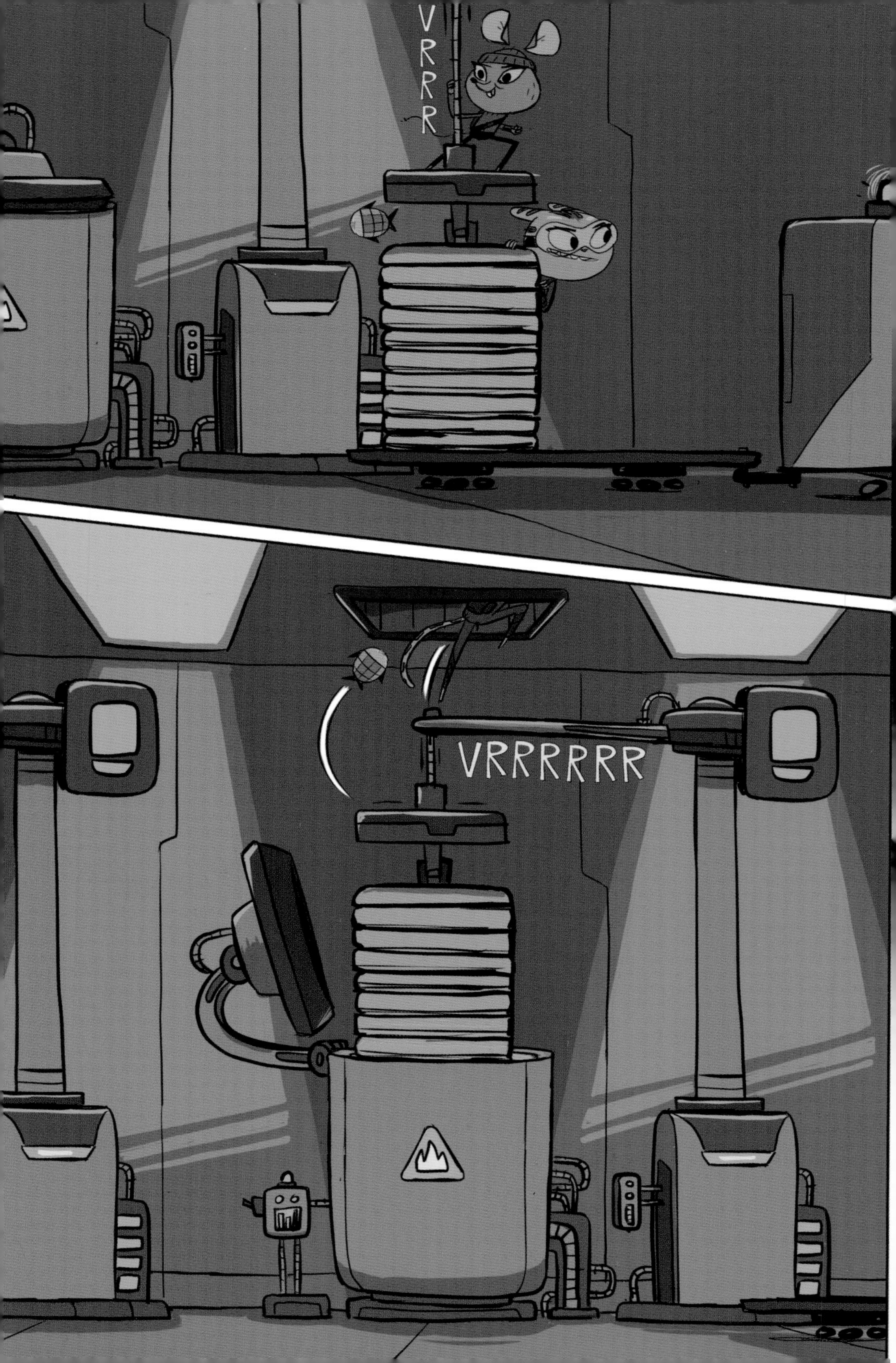
VRRR
VRRRRRR

BZT
BZT
STAMP
ZRRR
ZRRR

SKiPPeR's
Fish-Flavored Yogurt
PLINK
PLINK
PLINK

HOP HOP

RESEARCH
RESEARCH
HOP HOP HOP
BEEP
CLICK
CLICK

YES! THE BATTERY'S STILL HERE.

MROW!

WE DID IT!

WE BEAT THE WOLF!

WHO'S THE BEST NOW?

NOT THE WOLF.
BECAUSE HE'S NOT HERE.

YA-HA-HA-HA-HA HAAAAAAAAAA!!

OH. HI. DID I SAY ALL THAT OUT LOUD?

ALL THAT'S LEFT TO DO NOW IS GRAB THE BATTERY AND GET OUT OF HERE.

WAIT!

THAT'S A PRESSURE PLATE.
IF WE LIFT THE BATTERY, IT'LL SET OFF THE ALARM.

WHAT'S OUR PLAN?
WE NEED TO FIND SOME-THING THAT WEIGHS THE SAME TO REPLACE THE BATTERY.

BEOOP.
ARE YOU SURE?
YOU RAN THE NUMBERS, AND THAT'S OUR ONLY CHOICE?

BEOOP.
SIGH... THAT'S BOTH CONVENIENT AND EXTREMELY DISAPPOINTING.

Thanks

WELP, THE MISSION DIDN'T GO EXACTLY TO PLAN, BUT AT LEAST WE STOPPED DIVISION FROM COMPLETING THE MCD.

I SAY THAT'S A WIN.

HEY, UH, THANKS FOR YOUR HELP.
NO THANKS NECESSARY. IT WAS A TEAM EFFORT.

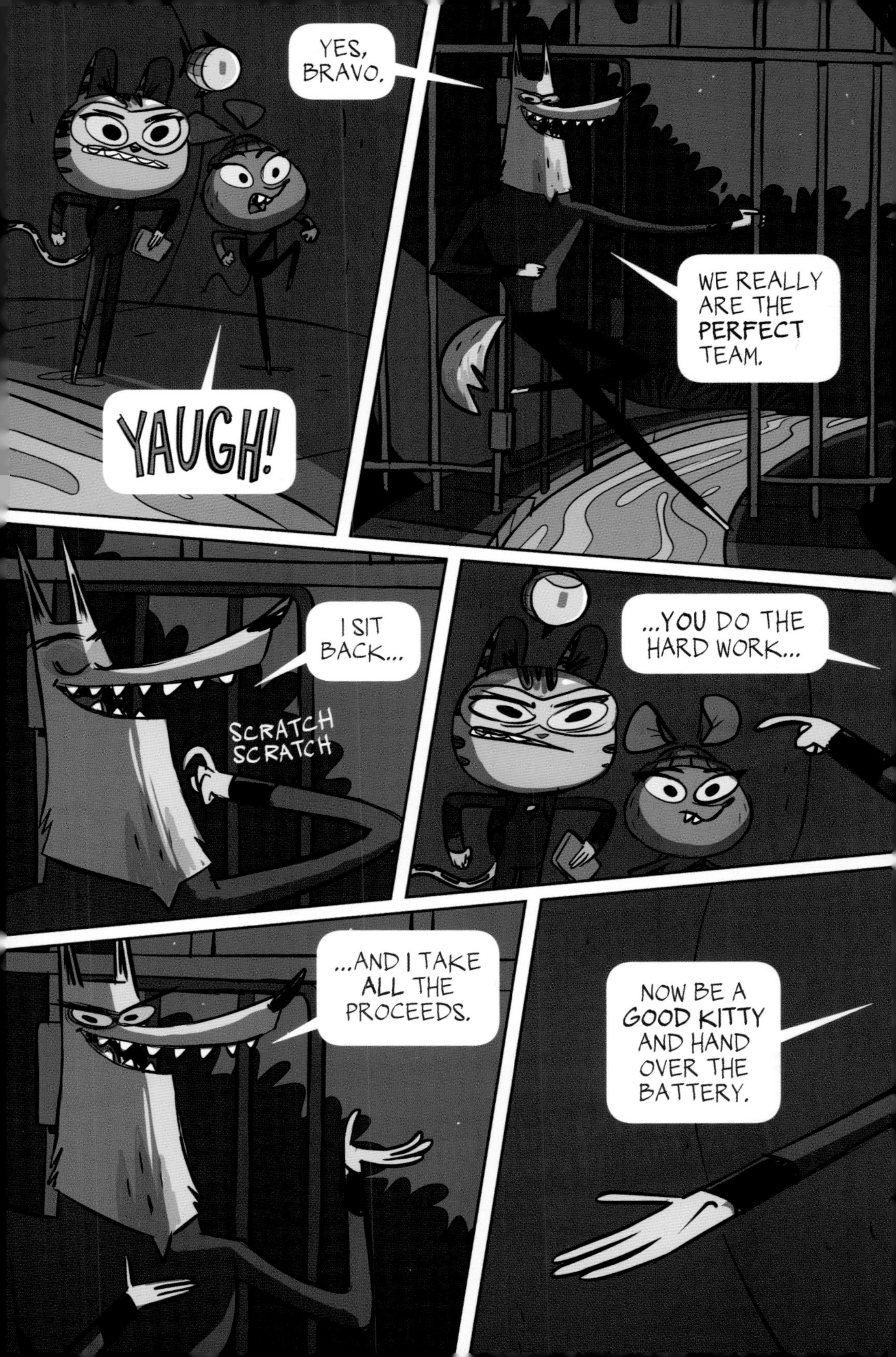
YES, BRAVO.
YAUGH!
WE REALLY ARE THE PERFECT TEAM.
I SIT BACK...
SCRATCH SCRATCH
...YOU DO THE HARD WORK...
...AND I TAKE ALL THE PROCEEDS.
NOW BE A GOOD KITTY AND HAND OVER THE BATTERY.

I'LL DESTROY THE BATTERY BEFORE I EVER GIVE IT TO YOU.
YAWN.
GO RIGHT AHEAD.
BUT YOU MIGHT WANT TO READ THE WARNING LABEL FIRST.
WARNING! THIS BATTERY HAS THE POWER TO LEVEL AN ENTIRE CITY. DO NOT DESTROY.

THAT'S AN ODDLY SPECIFIC WARNING LABEL.
ONCE AGAIN, IT APPEARS I HAVE OUTSMARTED YOU, AGENT 9.
BUT DON'T BEAT YOURSELF UP.

YOU JUST DON'T HAVE WHAT IT TAKES TO BE THE S4 AGENT THAT I USED TO BE.

WHAT?! YOU WERE NEVER AN S4 AGENT!

O DIDN'T TELL YOU?
HOW DELIGHTFUL.

HE PROBABLY DIDN'T WANT YOU TO FEEL LIKE A FAILURE, CONSTANTLY COMPARING YOURSELF TO ME.

OR MAYBE YOU AREN'T WORTH REMEMBERING.
RAUGH!
GIVE ME THE BATTERY!!

IF YOU WANT IT, YOU'LL HAVE TO TAKE IT FROM ME.
Q
BUT I DON'T THINK YOU CAN.
GRAB

HA-HA-HAAA!
THAT'S FUNNY!
GET READY.
GUM POD!
WHAT?!
STICK

YOU'RE GOING TO NEED MORE THAN GUM TO STOP ME, AGENT 9!

WHAT NOW?
BEOOP.
FIN'S RIGHT. THAT GUM WON'T HOLD HIM FOR LONG.
SLAM
BZZZ

WE NEED TO GET THIS BATTERY SOMEWHERE SAFE!
WHERE THE WOLF CAN'T GET HIS PAWS ON IT.
MAYBE WE CAN BORROW A CAR FROM THE PARKING LOT.
GOOD IDEA!

FASTEN YOUR SEAT BELT.
CLICK
CLICK

TURN
REE
RE
REE
RE

SPUTTER
SPUTTER
SPUTTER

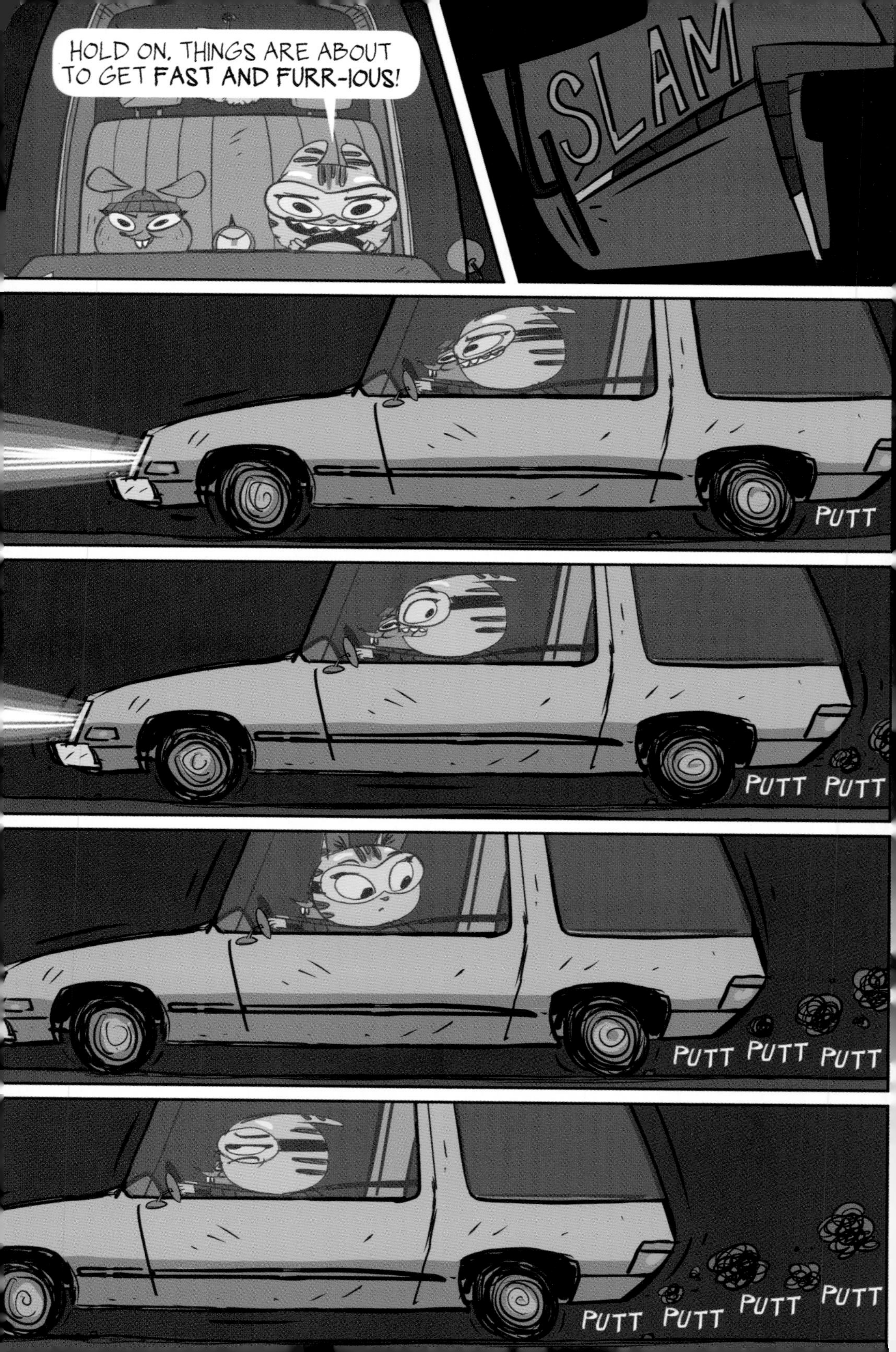
HOLD ON. THINGS ARE ABOUT TO GET FAST AND FURR-IOUS!
SLAM
PUTT
PUTT PUTT
PUTT PUTT PUTT
PUTT PUTT PUTT PUTT

QuarK LABS
COME ON!
GO, CAR, GO!
PUTT
PUTT
PUTT
PUTT
PUTT
PUTT

PUTT

PUTT
PUTT

SKREEEEEEE

SHOULD WE CALL HEADQUARTERS AND ARRANGE A PICKUP?
THAT'LL HAVE TO WAIT.
RAHHHH
WE'VE GOT COMPANY.
RAHHHHHHH
RAHHHH
WE'LL NEVER OUTRUN HIM IN THIS CAR.
TIME FOR EVASIVE MANEUVERS!
RAAAAHHHHHHH
SWERVE

PUTT PUTT PUTT PUTT
SKREEEEEEE
SKID

GUH GUH GUH GUH
RATTLE RATTLE
RATTLE
TURN

PUTT PUTT PUTT
RAHHHH
HONK!

RAHHHHHHHHHHH
SKREEECH
RAHHHH
SKREEECH

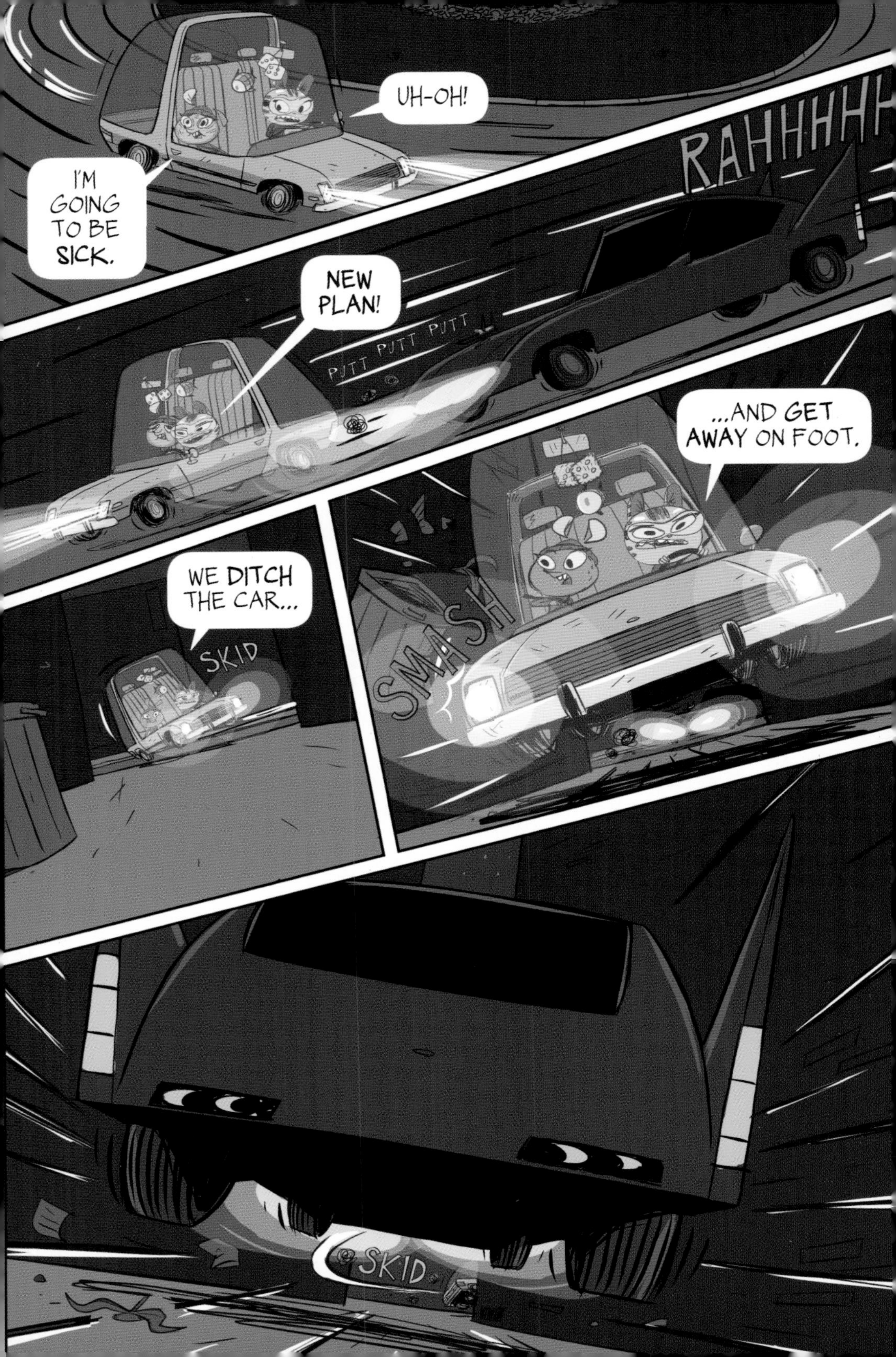

UH-OH!
I'M GOING TO BE SICK.
RAHHHHH
NEW PLAN!
PUTT PUTT PUTT
WE DITCH THE CAR...
SKID
...AND GET AWAY ON FOOT.
SMASH
SKID

WE CAN LOSE HIM IN THERE!
CONDEMNED
KEEP OUT
NO TRESPASSING
SKREECH

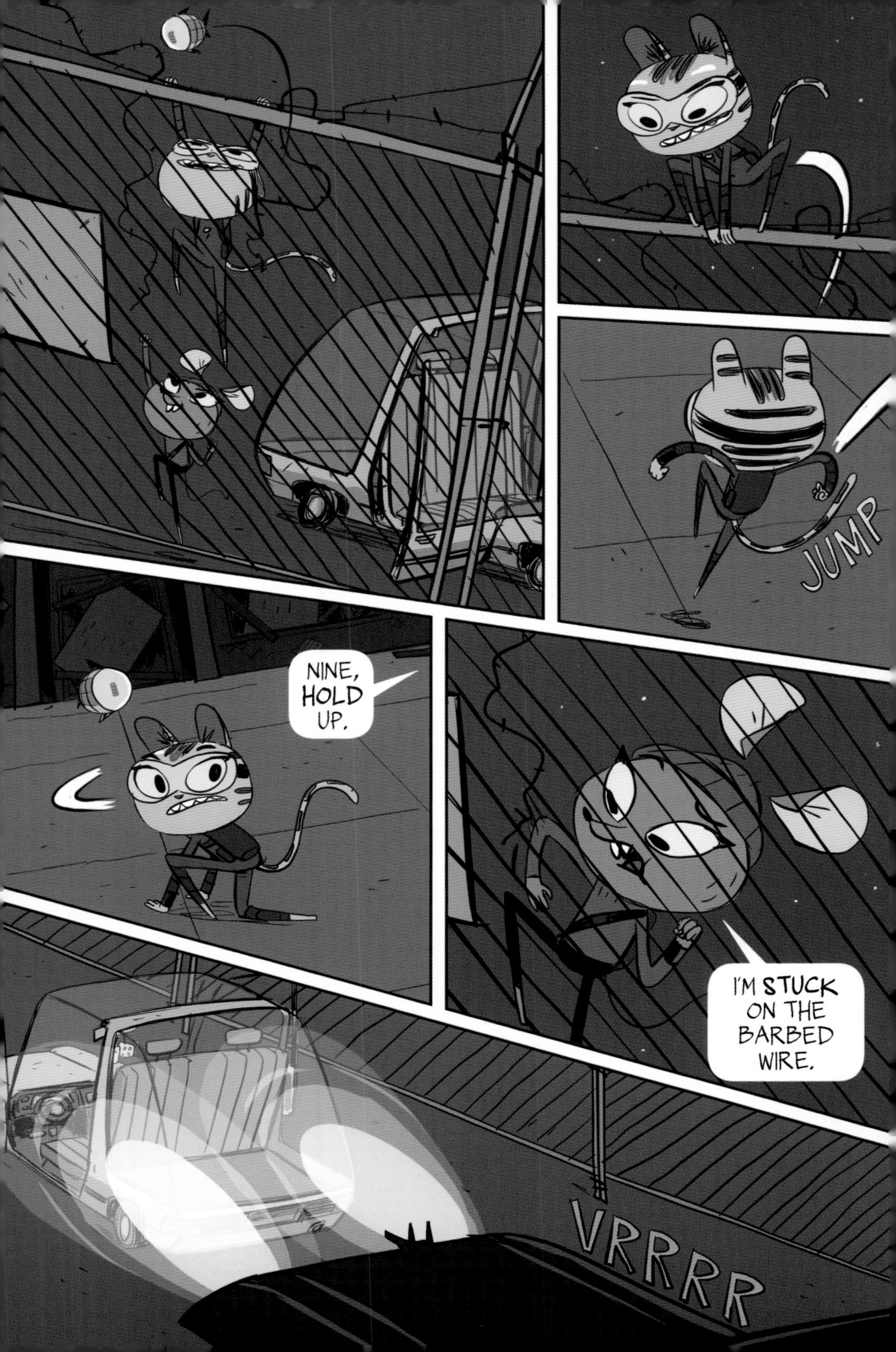
JUMP
NINE, HOLD UP.
I'M STUCK ON THE BARBED WIRE.
VRRRRR

NEED A HAND?
GRAB
LET HER GO!
HOW ABOUT A TRADE? THE MOUSE FOR THE BATTERY.

DON'T DO IT, NINE! GO ON WITHOUT ME.

IT LOOKS LIKE YOU HAVE A CHOICE TO MAKE.

DO YOU WANT TO SAVE THE WORLD?

OR SAVE THE MOUSE?

UUUUUUGH...
WHAT KIND OF AGENT ARE YOU?
PATHETIC OR UNSTOPPABLE?
HERE.
TAKE IT.

THAT'S THE DIFFERENCE BETWEEN YOU AND ME, AGENT 9.
I WOULD HAVE SAVED THE WORLD.
RAAAAAA

I CAN'T BELIEVE THIS.
MRRUAUGH!
TING
NOW WE'VE LOST BOTH ITEMS!
AND WE HAVE NO CLUE WHERE THE WOLF IS GOING!
SIGH... THIS MISSION IS A TOTAL FAILURE.

UH... I KNOW WHERE HE'S GOING.

OR AT LEAST I WILL WHEN HE GETS THERE WITH THE MICRO-TRACKING CHIP I STUCK ON HIS BACK.

SEE?
THE WOLF

YOU ARE A GENIUS!

I MEAN...
EXCELLENT WORK, AGENT TRAPS.

LET'S RIDE!
SLIIDE
THUD

POP

LET'S DO THAT AGAIN.
SLIIDE

SORRY.
HAD TO GET THAT RIGHT.

TURN
CLICK
CLICK
CLICK
CLICK
CLICK

NO!
C'MON, CAR. NOW IS **NOT** THE TIME TO **QUIT** ON US!!

NOT AFTER ALL THE **MILES** WE'VE GONE TOGETHER.
TURN
CLICK
CLICK
CLICK

BEEEEE
I'M AFRAID IT'S **LOST** THE WILL TO DRIVE.
THUNK

SHOULD I CALL ROTORS?
DEFINITELY!

A BIT LATER...
SLIIIIDE
SLIIIIDE

DIVISION—SECRET LAB

YOU'RE MAKING A HUGE MISTAKE.
YOU CAN'T DOUBLE-CROSS DIVISION AND EXPECT TO GET AWAY WITH IT.
THAT'S WHERE YOU'RE WRONG.
NOW THAT I HAVE THIS, EVERYONE'S MIND WILL BE UNDER MY CONTROL.
WELL, TECHNICALLY, IT ONLY WORKS ON ONE MIND AT A TIME.

BEOOP.
IT'S TOO LATE. BY THE TIME SUPPORT GETS HERE, THE WOLF WILL BE GONE.
WE NEED TO END THIS, HERE AND NOW.
ARE YOU SURE THAT'S POSSIBLE?
WE'VE GOT THE ELEMENT OF SURPRISE ON OUR SIDE.
ALL YOU AND FIN HAVE TO DO IS SNEAK IN THROUGH THE WINDOW WHILE I ATTACK FROM THE ELEVATOR.
WHAT ABOUT THE MIND-CONTROL—
I'LL KEEP THE WOLF OCCUPIED WHILE YOU AND FIN DESTROY THE DEVICE!
BUT WHAT IF HE USES IT ON US?
HE WON'T HAVE A CHANCE.

DING
EXPECTING SOMEONE?
NO. I DON'T GET MANY VISITORS, AND MY SECRET LOCATION PRETTY MUCH MAKES FOOD DELIVERY IMPOSSIBLE.
OPEN
SSSSSSSSS
I'M GOING TO GUESS THAT'S FOR YOU.
THAT'S OFF MY CAR!!
SSST

YAAAUU

YOU'RE UNDER MY CONTROL NOW, AGENT 9!
BZAP

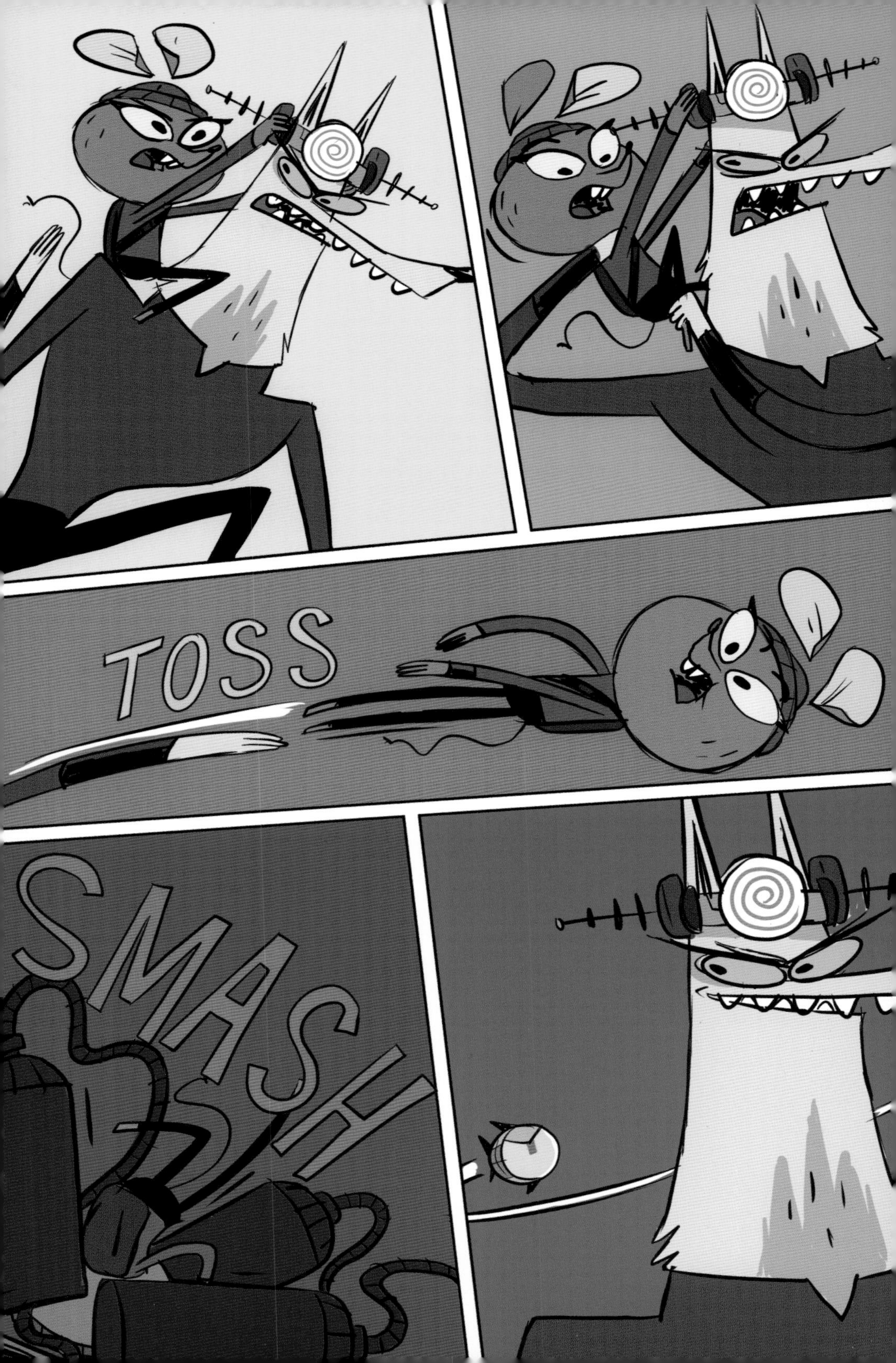
TOSS
SMASH

BZZ
GRAB
BEOOP.
BZOOo
TURN
CLANK

HOWL!

SOON I WILL HAVE
MY REVENGE!

EXCUSE ME.

HI. SORRY TO INTERRUPT YOUR BIG MOMENT.

IS REVENGE REALLY WORTH ALL THIS TROUBLE?

I MEAN, WOULDN'T YOU RATHER HAVE A COOL BEANIE INSTEAD?

I COULD KNIT YOU ONE IN EXCHANGE FOR THE MIND-CONTROL DEVICE.

WHAT DO YA SAY? LIGHT BLUE TO MATCH YOUR EYES.
IT MIGHT SOFTEN YOUR GRUFF APPEARENCE AND MAKE YOU SEEM MORE LIKABLE.
GRRRR.

I HAVE A BETTER IDEA.
HOW ABOUT WE PLAY A LITTLE GAME OF CAT AND MOUSE?
WINNER GETS THE MIND-CONTROL DEVICE.
I'VE PLAYED THAT MANY TIMES BEFORE. IT'S NOT AS FUN AS YOU MIGHT THINK.
BRING ME THE MOUSE!
TIME TO RUN!

SLIDE
NINE, IT'S ME, TRAPS!
SWIPE
YAGH!
REMEMBER, WE BOTH LIKE FISH-FLAVORED YOGURT.
YOU SAID IT HAS "JUST THE RIGHT AMOUNT OF SALTY GOODNESS."
NEVER MIND!
TOSS

LAND
BONK
MROW!
SORRY!

HUH? HOW DID I—
HEY! THE MIND-CONTROL SIGNAL DIDN'T W—
WHOA!
TRIP
THIS IS NOT GOUDA.

I'D SAY THAT O HAS REALLY **FAILED** AS THE HEAD OF **S4**.

WOULDN'T YOU AGREE?

AGENTS SHOULD BE **RUTHLESS**!
THEY SHOULD BE **FEARED**!
WILLING TO DO **WHATEVER** IT TAKES TO COMPLETE A MISSION.
NOT AN **EASILY** DEFEATED, **GUM-THROWING** SEWING CIRCLE.
JUST TO CLARIFY— **IT'S KNITTING**.

GRRR.
BUT **SEWING** WORKS TOO.

WELL, THINGS ARE ABOUT TO CHANGE.

IT'S TIME FOR ME TO GO SEE AN **OLD FRIEND.**

STICK

BEEP
5:00

GOOD-BYE, AGENT 9.
THANKS FOR ALL YOUR **HELP.**

CLOSE
BEEP
4:53

ERGH. COME ON! WE CAN STILL STOP HIM.
NO.

YOU GO AHEAD.
I CAN'T DO IT.

I DID EVERYTHING WRONG.
THE WOLF IS RIGHT.

I'M PATHETIC.
I DON'T BELONG IN S4.

WHAT? YOU CAN'T LET THAT FLEABAG INTO YOUR HEAD.
IT'S TOO LATE FOR THAT.

BONK
NO! IT'S NOT.
OW.
WHY'D YOU DO THAT?

BECAUSE I REFUSE TO LET YOU GIVE UP.
SO HERE'S...
THE NEW PLAN!
FIRST, WE ARE GOING TO GET RID OF THIS BOMB.
3:45
BEEP
THEN WE'LL CALL O AND TELL HIM WE HAD A MINOR SETBACK.

THEN WE'LL TRACK DOWN THE WOLF TOGETHER AND...
GNA GNA GNA
GNA GNA GNA
SAVE THE WORLD!
WHAT DO YOU SAY? ARE YOU IN?
I'M IN.
OH, WAIT. YOU WEREN'T TALKING TO ME, WERE YOU? THIS IS EMBARRASSING. JUST PRETEND I DIDN'T SAY ANYTHING.

I SAY THIS MISSION ISN'T OVER YET!
LET'S GO!
WAIT! I NEED TO UNTIE YOU.
THERE'S NO TIME!
NOW THAT'S THE NINE I KNOW.
BEEP
0:47
BEEP
JUMP
GRAB
BEEP
WHAT DO YOU NEED ME TO DO?
OPEN THE WINDOW!
ON IT!

BEEP
BEEP
BEEP
OPEN
BEEP
BEEP
BEEP

KICK
BEEP
BEEP
BEEP
BEEP
BEEP
BOOM

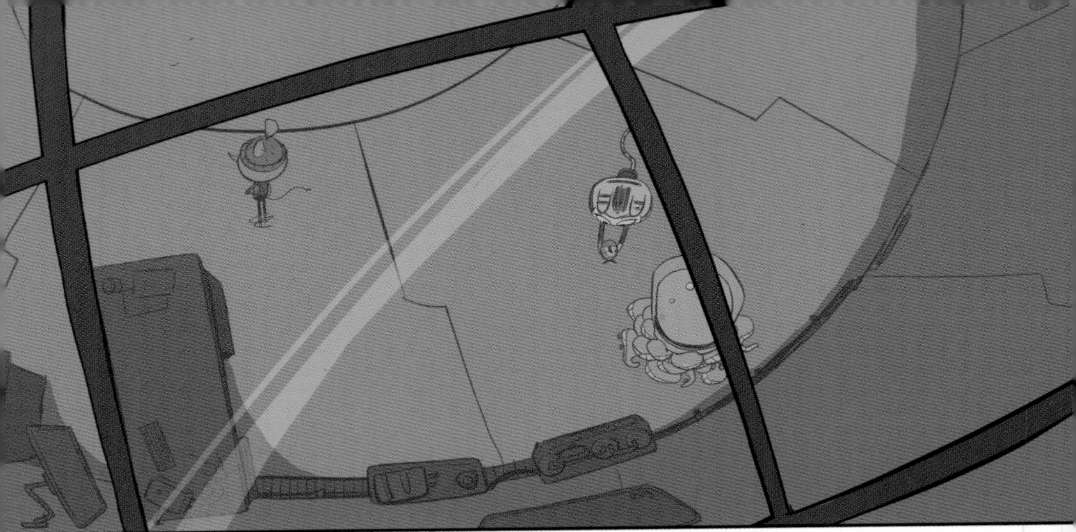

HEY, BUDDY.
SORRY FOR POWERING YOU DOWN.
BEOOP?
TURN
NO. HE GOT AWAY. BUT WE'RE GOING TO FIND HIM.

BEOOP?
YES. AND WE'LL FIGURE OUT A WAY TO **BLOCK** THE MIND-CONTROL SIGNAL.

WE JUST NEED TO KNOW HOW THE SIGNAL WAS BLOCKED INSIDE THERE.

I COULD KNIT YOU SOME MITTENS IN EXCHANGE FOR YOUR HELP.
OOOOH! MY TENTACLES DO GET A TAD CHILLY OUTSIDE THE WATER.
YOU SEE, YOU CAN'T BLOCK THE SIGNAL, BUT YOU CAN REDIRECT IT AROUND OBJECTS USING AN IRON, NICKEL, OR COBALT MICROMESH.
WELL, THAT'S ONE PROBLEM SOLVED.
BEOOP.
YUUGHH. YOU'RE RIGHT.
I STILL NEED TO CALL HQ AND TELL O EVERYTHING.
HE'S NOT GOING TO BE HAPPY.

BUT ON THE PLUS SIDE, YOU DON'T HAVE TO DO IT ALONE THIS TIME.
AND I'LL BE HERE TOO IF YOU NEED ME.

AGENT 9. TRAPS. I WAS WONDERING WHEN I'D HEAR FROM YOU.
I **ASSUME** THAT THINGS DID **NOT** GO TO PLAN.

YOU WOULD BE CORRECT IN THAT ASSUMPTION.
SCRATCH SCRATCH

BUT THE **GOOD NEWS** IS... WE FOUND THE LAB AND CAPTURED **IQ**.

SEE!
HI. NICE TO MEET YOU.

AND I ASSUME YOU ALSO HAVE **BAD NEWS**.

THAT DEPENDS ON WHAT YOU CONSIDER BAD NEWS.

IF IT'S THE WOLF GETTING AWAY WITH A WORKING MIND-CONTROL DEVICE—

AND THE TRACKING CHIP WE PLACED ON HIM NO LONGER WORKING...
THEN YES, WE HAVE BAD NEWS.

IT DOES SOUND LIKE BAD NEWS TO ME.

BUT AS A **TEAM-BUILDING** EXERCISE, THINGS WENT **EXCEPTIONALLY** WELL.
THERE'S NO "I" IN TEAM.

RUB
RUB
AT LEAST THE MISSION WASN'T A **COMPLETE** FAILURE.

I'LL SEND A RETRIEVAL UNIT, AND WE CAN MEET BACK AT **HEADQUARTERS** IN THE MORNING TO DISCUSS NEXT STEPS.

GOOD-NIGHT.
BZP

EITHER THAT WENT WELL, OR O WAS **TOO TIRED** TO GET UPSET.
DEFINITELY THE LATTER.

THE NEXT DAY...
YUCK'S
PICKLED BRUSSELS SPROUTS
S4 HEADQUARTERS

GOOD DAY, E! YOU'RE LOOKING FIT AS EVER.

GOT YOUR FAVORITE DRINK—LUKEWARM MATCHA GREEN TEA.

HOW'S O TODAY? IS HE IN A GOOD MOOD?
O'S OUT. HE CALLED IN SICK.

DID HE ASK YOU TO RESCHEDULE OUR MORNING MEETING?

NOPE. ALL HE SAID WAS "I'M NOT FEELING WELL," AND HUNG UP.

O DID LOOK TIRED WHEN WE SPOKE TO HIM LAST NIGHT.
HE ALWAYS LOOKS LIKE THAT AFTER I CALL HIM.

SOMETHING DOESN'T FEEL RIGHT. O DOESN'T FLAKE ON MEETINGS...

IT'S JUST ONE SICK DAY.
AND HE HASN'T MISSED A SINGLE DAY OF WORK IN TWENTY-FIVE YEARS.

HERE. I'LL PROVE IT.

LOOK. TWENTY-FIVE YEARS.
OKAY. I SEE YOUR POINT. SOMETHING DOES SEEM ODD.
25 YEARS OF PERFECT SERVICE

HEY.

DISAVOWED

DO YOU THINK O NOT SHOWING UP HAS SOMETHING TO DO WITH THE WOLF?
DISAVOWED

IT SAYS HERE HE WAS KICKED OUT OF S4.

WAIT. DIDN'T THE WOLF SAY HE WAS GOING TO SEE AN OLD FRIEND?
GASP!
O'S THE OLD FRIEND!
I KNOW WHERE THE WOLF IS!

WHY ARE WE YELLING?

GLAD WE GOT...
THAT OUT OF OUR SYSTEM.

FROM HERE ON OUT, WE GOT THIS!

WHERE DO WE START?
I'M OPEN TO ANY AND ALL SUGGESTIONS AS LONG AS WE END UP WITH A CAT-PROOF PLAN TO RESCUE O.

FIRST, WE NEED TO MAKE SURE O IS STILL AT HOME AND THAT THE WOLF HASN'T TAKEN HIM SOMEWHERE ELSE.

WE'LL GET SURVEILLANCE ON THAT RIGHT AWAY.

BEOOP.
DEFINITELY. WE DON'T WANT ANY MINDS COMPROMISED THIS TIME AROUND.
I'LL GET S4 TECH TO MAKE THE MIND-CONTROL SIGNAL DEFLECTORS IQ SUGGESTED.
I'LL DOWNLOAD THE BLUEPRINTS FOR O'S HOME AND FIND A WAY FOR US TO GET IN UNDETECTED.
AND WHILE YOU'RE DOING THAT, FIN AND I WILL FIGURE OUT HOW TO GET O OUT.

THEN THAT JUST LEAVES THE WOLF.
LEAVE HIM TO ME.

O'S COUNTRY MANOR—LATER...

WE'VE GOT EYES ON THE INSIDE!

BZZZZ

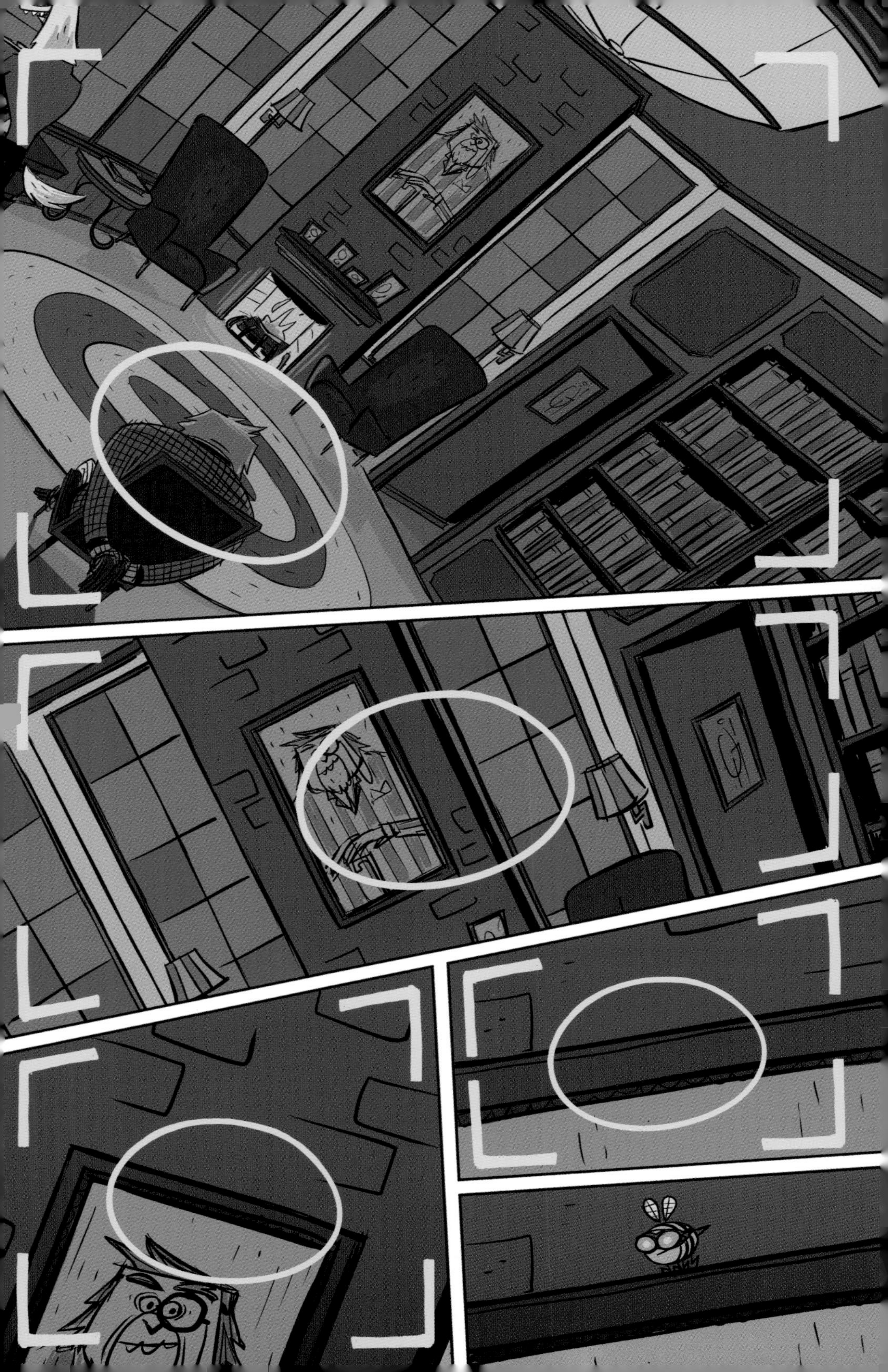

IT'S UNBELIEVABLE THAT AFTER ALL THESE YEARS, YOU CAN'T LET IT GO—
YOU HAD NO RIGHT TO REMOVE ME FROM S4.
YOU BROUGHT THAT ON YOURSELF. YOU WERE ARROGANT.
AND NEVER CARED WHO GOT HURT AS LONG AS YOU CAME OUT ON TOP.

THAT'S RIGHT. AND SOON, WITH YOUR HELP...

...I'LL BE TOP DOG AT S4.

IS EVERYONE CLEAR ON WHAT YOU'RE SUPPOSED TO DO?
BEOOP!
ALL CHEESED UP AND READY!
OPERATION DISAPPEAR-O IS A GO!

I'M IN POSITION.
I'M GOING IN.
BEOOP.
CREAK

ASK

ASK
FLEABAG

FOR

COUGH! COUGH!!

COUGH! COUGH!
COUGH!
COUGH!
COUGH!
COUGH!
COUGH!
DO YOU MIND?

SORRY—COUGH! I'VE GOT A—COUGH! COUGH! TICKLE IN MY THROAT—COUGH!

FINE. I'LL GET YOU SOME WATER.
COUGH!
COUGH!

WE'RE GOING TO MAKE YOU DISAPPEAR.
BE READY.

GNA GNA GNA

GNA GNA

HERE.
SNIFF
SNIFF
PING

BZZOOOOOOOOooo

RAUGH! I KNEW IT!

BLIP
HI! HOW ARE YA?
MISS ME MUCH?
AGENT 9!
I JUST CAN'T SEEM TO GET RID OF YOU!
NOPE.
YOU MUST NOT BE AS GOOD AS YOU THINK YOU ARE.
I COMMAND YOU TO BRING ME O!

UHHHH...
NO.

YOU'RE UNDER MY CONTROL.
I SAID, "BRING ME O!"

YAWN.
I'M NOT YOUR PUPPET. DO IT YOURSELF.

WHAT'S WRONG WITH THIS THING?

YOUR LITTLE TOY ISN'T GOING TO WORK ANYMORE, THANKS TO MY NEW MICROMESH, SIGNAL-DEFLECTING BEANIE.

IQ WAS MORE THAN HAPPY TO HELP US IN EXCHANGE FOR SOME KNITTED MITTENS.

PROBABLY NOT THE SMARTEST IDEA TO DOUBLE-CROSS THE OCTOPUS WHO MADE YOUR TECH.
YOU MAY HAVE FOUND A WAY TO STOP THE MIND-CONTROL DEVICE, BUT YOU CAN'T STOP ME.
THAT'S WHERE WE MAY HAVE A DIFFERENCE OF OPINION.
HA! I'M EVERYTHING YOU'LL NEVER BE.
TOSS
I'M THE BEST.
AND YOU'RE WEAK-MINDED AND PATHETIC!

HERE'S THE THING, WOLFY.
I DON'T HAVE TO BE THE BEST TO BEAT YOU.
I JUST NEED TO KNOW WHEN TO ASK FOR HELP.
WHAT?!
AND WORK WITH THE BEST TEAM.
NO!

NO!
LOOKS LIKE YOU'RE TRAPPED!
WHICH MEANS... MISSION ACCOMPLISHED!

HEADQUARTERS
S4
THE NEXT DAY...
OPERATION:
MIND CONTROL!
COMPLETED
CONGRATULATIONS, YOU THREE.
THE MISSION ENDED UP BEING A SUCCESS AFTER ALL.

I ALSO WANT TO THANK YOU FOR COMING TO MY RESCUE.
AND FOR NOT DESTROYING MY HOME IN THE PROCESS.

BUT, JUST TO BE CLEAR, THERE'S A GOOD CHANCE I WILL DESTROY STUFF ON FUTURE MISSIONS.

IT'S BEST TO KEEP YOUR EXPECTATIONS LOW.
OH, YES. I KNOW.

I'D SAY WE MAKE AN EXCELLENT TEAM, WOULDN'T YOU?
DEFINITELY.

HOPEFULLY WE CAN WORK TOGETHER AGAIN IN THE FUTURE.
BEOOP.
I WOULDN'T MIND THAT.

THIS CALLS FOR A CELEBRATORY SNACK.

FISH-FLAVORED YOGURT FOR EVERYONE!

FOLLOW ME TO THE CAFETERIA!
UH, I'LL STICK TO MY USUAL DURIAN FRUIT FLAVOR.

SPY OF THE MONTH

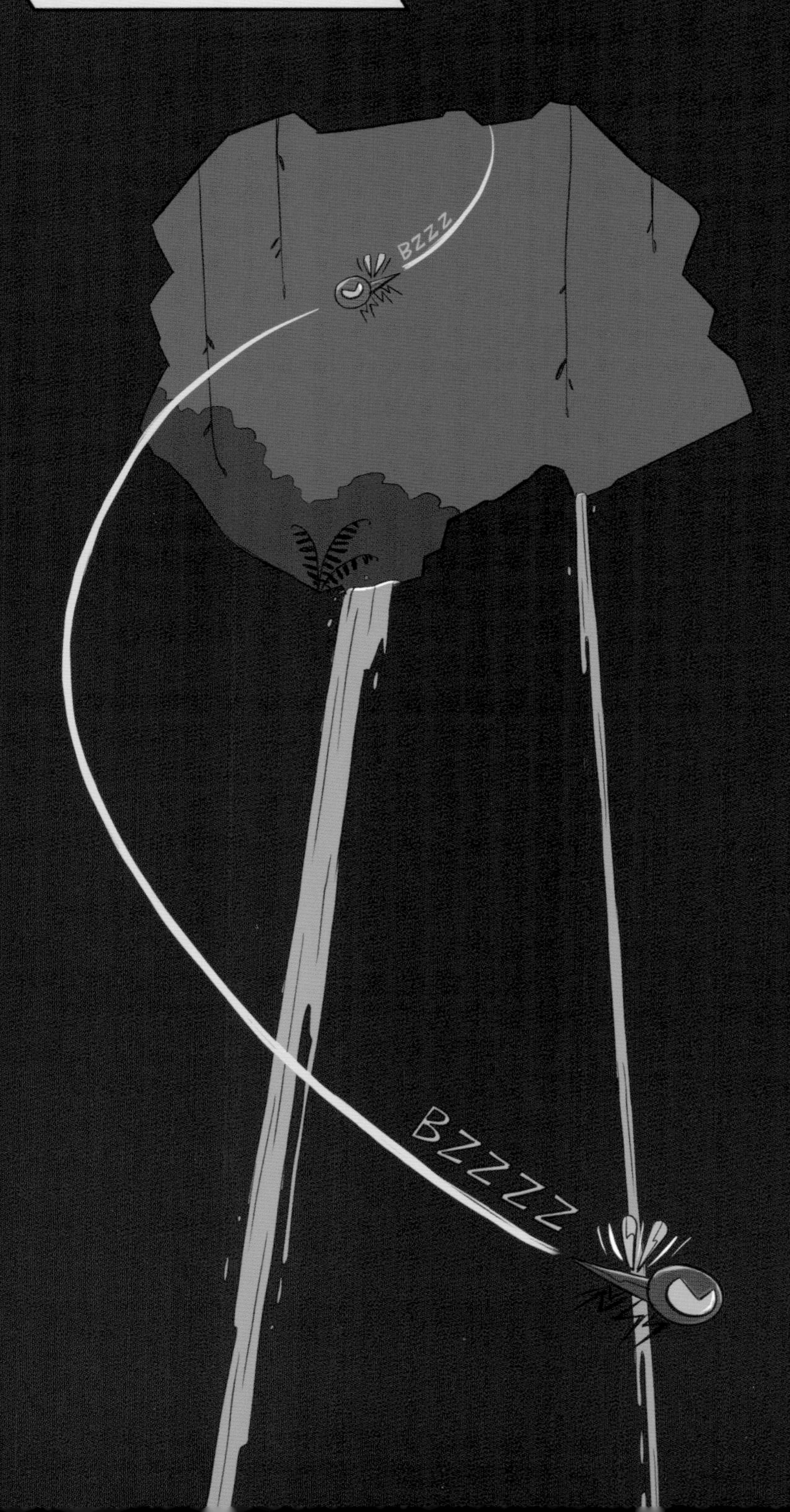
DIVISION—SECRET LAIR
BZZZ
BZZZZZ

BZZZZ
BZZZ

WELL, WELL, WELL...
IT APPEARS I NOW HAVE TWO THINGS ON MY TO-DO LIST.
TAKE OVER THE WORLD...
...AND ELIMINATE AGENT 9!
THE END